Praise for Traci Hall's
Her Wiccan, Wiccan Ways

"...A little scary, some romance with a paranormal twist. This is a great debut in the new young adult series about psychic prodigy Rhiannon Godfrey...This book will have you bewitched from the first chapter and put a spell on you...with twists and turns in the story to keep you hooked...this is truly a magical read...luckily there is a sequel 'Something Wiccan This Way Comes' and hopefully it won't be a long wait until it is released."

  ~ *Amber Chalmers, ParaNormal Romance*

"...Rhiannon Godfrey a psychic prodigy from a family of Wiccans I really like Rhiannon's character, she is tough, spirited, and even though she struggles she knows what the right thing to do is... Her Wiccan, Wiccan Ways is a great start for this new young adult series. I am looking forward to the second book. If you enjoy young adult fiction with all the angst of being a teenager and a paranormal twist, you will also enjoy this book."

  ~ *Steph B., The Romance Studio*

Look for these titles by
Traci Hall

Now Available:

Rhiannon Godfrey Series:
Her Wiccan, Wiccan Ways (Book 1)
Something Wiccan This Way Comes (Book 2)

Her Wiccan, Wiccan Ways

Traci Hall

A Samhain Publishing, Ltd. publication.

Samhain Publishing, Ltd.
577 Mulberry Street, Suite 1520
Macon, GA 31201
www.samhainpublishing.com

Her Wiccan, Wiccan Ways
Copyright © 2008 by Traci Hall
Print ISBN: 978-1-60504-104-9
Digital ISBN: 1-59998-910-7

Editing by Lindsey McGurk
Cover by Scott Carpenter

First Samhain Publishing, Ltd. electronic publication: April 2008
First Samhain Publishing, Ltd. print publication: December 2008

Dedication

For Greg, Bri and Des—and all my family and friends. The road to publication has been long (very, very long), but your support never wavered!

In memory of Loren—thanks for always believing.

Chapter One

Rhiannon Godfrey turned up the volume on her iPod, blocking out her mother's annoying attempts to get inside her head.

Starla Godfrey was nothing if not persistent.

The noise was like the buzzing of a bee trapped between a screen and a window; buzz-buzz-buzzing until finally she just couldn't stand it anymore.

Rhiannon yanked off her headphones and yelled, "Helllooo? Dr. Richards told you to respect my boundaries."

Her mother turned around from the front passenger seat of the car. "Yes, well, Dr. Richards hasn't been trying to get your attention for the past thirty minutes."

Rhiannon rolled her eyes. "I was listening to my music." She exhaled certain that she had the worst possible life in the entire world. Maybe even the universe. "What do you *want?*"

"That's enough, Rhee."

She glared at the back of her father's head, his dark hair barely visible over the back of the driver's seat. Was she telepathically strong enough to make him turn the car around and head back to Vegas?

He stiffened, met her gaze in the rearview mirror and said sternly, "Knock it off, Rhiannon."

She plopped back in her seat. It had been worth a try.

"Is it too much for you to look out the window?" Her mom pointed toward the passing scenery. "To take joy in your surroundings?"

"Yeah, it is too much. This isn't vacation, we aren't exactly touring the seven flippin' wonders of the world. You are ruining my life! Moving me to Crystal Lake, Washington, home of the dairy cow."

Her mom pressed her lips tightly together, and Rhiannon could practically hear her mother's silent prayer to the Goddess for patience. But unlike Starla, Rhee just didn't go barging around in people's heads uninvited.

"We researched Crystal Lake. It is small, homey, and perfect for us to get back to our roots."

Crossing her arms, Rhee replied in what she thought was a calm and reasonable voice, "Mom. I want to go back to the institute. To my friends. *You're* the one who is excited about fresh eggs straight from a chicken's butt, which is so completely gross that I am never eating eggs again. It was *your* stupid idea to move us all the way from civilization to open a New Age shop in an old barn, where the good citizens of Crystal Lake are probably going to burn us all at the stake for witchcraft."

"Rhee!"

Rhiannon stopped bobbing her foot against the back of her dad's seat. When he raised his voice, he meant business. But she had *so* much more to say—like how unfair this move was, and how rotten living in the country was going to be. She was a *city* girl.

She swallowed past the lump in her throat as she thought of the institute lounge where she, Tanya, and Matthew liked to spend their afternoons. Her eyes burned with stupid tears but she blinked them away furiously. There was no way she was crying, again, in front of her parents.

"Stop staring at me, Mom." Rhee tilted her chin defiantly in the air.

Sympathy and concern floated back from the front seat of the car like a too-sweet perfume, making her squirm with guilt. Okay, so maybe she had been a little mean.

But she wasn't gonna apologize! Everything she'd said was true.

Her mother murmured, "This move was for the good of the family, which you are a part of. It isn't like you to sulk and pout, Rhiannon. We are going forward, you should have your arms outstretched to embrace the future. I know that you will miss your friends, but you'll make new ones."

Rhee flinched. She didn't want new friends, it had been hard enough making the old ones. Her mom *so* didn't get it.

"You're going to go to a real school, high school! No more exhausting research experiments, no more CAT scans, flashcards or electrodes. You won't have to travel and get food poisoning, like that time you went to France. C'mon, honey, doesn't that excite you at all?"

She gulped. Her stomach clenched and she felt like she was gonna hurl, and it had nothing to do with food poisoning. She liked the institute, loved Dr. Richards and Mrs. Edwards, who had helped her deal with her stupid psychic abilities. And she'd had two super-great friends. Matthew, who actually lived at the Institute of Parapsychology, and Tanya, who was fourteen just like her, and came in the afternoons.

"I want to be home-schooled. I can take online pre-college courses."

Her mom shook her head and said in an unusually firm tone, "We've read your chart. The planets are aligned for change. Your soul needs to be around other kids your own age—regular people, Rhee—in order to realize its full potential."

She stared at her mom, thinking hard of her first day of kindergarten, the first time she'd realized she was practically an alien. She hadn't known that amusing her new classmates with floating pencils would send her nice teacher, Miss Hutchinson, into a tizzy, making her scream and faint, which then made all the other bratty kids start crying, and wham—she'd been sent home, labeled a freak. *No*, she thought as her stomach twisted again, the idea of school didn't excite her.

It made her sick.

Her mom frowned, having picked up Rhee's vision loud and clear. "It won't be that way. You're older now, it will be better this time." Her mom's voice sounded sad, which pleased Rhiannon to no end. Why should she be the only one suffering here?

Closing her eyes, she knew she didn't need to be a freakin' mind reader to know that her mom blamed herself for sending Rhiannon to Dr. Richards all those years ago. Starla hadn't counted on her daughter preferring logical science as an explanation for her strange and sometimes uncontrollable abilities.

Not when she, a second-generation Wiccan, put all her faith in miracles and magick.

Talk about needing to grow up! Rhee knew her mom still believed in unicorns, which was okay, like, when you were five or six, but *thirty*-six? Sheesh.

She opened her eyes and peeked out the window. Miles and miles of brown grass, lop-sided fences and cows. Dumb cows, just chewing their cud and watching the cars pass by.

Was this what her new life was going to be like? Stuck in the middle of Nowhere, USA?

Biting her lip, she knew the real reason behind the move,

even though her parents hadn't said it right out. Being older hadn't helped her control her impulses all that much, at least not when she lost her temper.

And it was that Maddie Johnson's entire stupid, idiotic fault.

Rhiannon stuck her headphones back over her ears and cranked The Donnas' latest single up full blast so that she could get some sleep. A girl had to pass the time somehow, and talking with her parents went way beyond lame.

She must have actually dozed off, because the light touch of her mom's hand tapping her on the leg jolted her from a dream.

"Wake up, honey! We're here! Oh, this is so exciting, look at the yard."

Her mom opened the door the minute the car was parked. Rhee stretched her arms over her head, a little groggy from being jerked out of sleep. She'd been dreaming...something *different.*

Blinking against the bright Washington sunshine, Rhee stumbled from the back seat of the car. She took a sec to soak up the energy from the summer sun's rays before looking around. Then she rubbed her eyes, certain her mind was playing tricks on her. The house—no, she quickly changed her mind—this was definitely an old farm, shimmered in front of her. She yawned, annoyed that she couldn't concentrate. *Why am I so tired? My eyelashes feel like they weigh five pounds each.*

She bit the inside of her cheek and brought the worn-down farmhouse into focus. Clarity didn't help. She winced with distaste at the warped porch. *Great, we bought a dump.* Which is what her mom deserved for choosing a house with "character" over a brand new one with a pool.

If character meant "in need of a paint job", then the farm fit the bill and her mom should be deliriously happy. Except— Rhee squinted to keep the farmhouse image from wavering—it had looked kept up in the pictures the realtor had sent. Pictures she'd studied behind her parents' backs, so that they wouldn't know she'd been even the tiniest bit interested in the house or dumb Crystal Lake. And wasn't the trim around the windows supposed to be yellow?

In fact, she was kinda surprised to see the walkway all cracked and filled with dead weeds. Hadn't the path been paved with bricks in the photos? Her chest tightened. *Why is it so hot?* Rhiannon ran her forearm across her forehead and licked her dry lips. This was ridiculous! She was from Las Vegas, Nevada and used to serious, sidewalk-melting heat. This puny Washington stuff shouldn't be getting to her. She swallowed, thirsty. The farmhouse flickered like a hologram.

I'm dreaming. She heard the far away sound of her mom saying something to her dad, but she couldn't make out the exact words, they were too fuzzy. She tried to step forward, but it was like she was all tangled up in her blankets. Rhee made herself open her eyes wide, using her fingers to keep them that way.

The white, supposed-to-be-sunshine-yellow trim was peeling around the windows and doors of the farmhouse. The front door was hanging on its hinges. She blinked, knowing for a fact the front door in the pictures had been white, with a decorative window at the top, not an unpainted wooden slab. *This is so not right.* Apprehension shot through her system, sending her psychic alarm on high alert, and she slowly looked up. Somehow Rhee knew she had to, even if she didn't want to.

And she really, *really* didn't want to. Her skin tingled and her gaze was being pulled up as if drawn by a powerful magnet. Sucking in a surprised breath, Rhiannon noticed the attic window was all broken and cracked, but that wasn't what made her feel like she was going to pee her pants. No. *That* would be the pale face with big, dark holes for eyes staring down at her through the jagged panes.

Rhiannon's scream stuck in her throat. She had to warn her parents that there was someone in the house, but all that came out was a squeak. Realization hit her like a speeding train. The dream-like feeling, her tiredness, her thirst...this was no dream. Not a nightmare either. She was having what Dr. Richards would call a "spontaneous psychic episode", which meant that she was wide-frickin'-awake.

And she was seeing her very first ghost.

Now what? Rhee could hardly have a panic attack, even though, from the way her pulse was racing, a part of her thought it was a good idea.

Shaking inside and out, she made herself think about what Dr. Richards would instruct her to do. Or Mrs. Edwards. Yeah, Mrs. Edwards was so famous that even the cops sometimes used her to help solve cases. She'd say in her Irish accented voice, "Pay attention, Rhiannon, luv. Look at the details."

She tried, but it felt like she had a penny taped to the top of each eyelid. It was as if someone was trying to hypnotize her or something.

Rhee had enough training against unwanted mental intrusions to be able to put up her defensive shields. Would they work against ghosts? Was she too late?

Focus, she thought, pinching the sensitive skin between her finger and her thumb, *on the features.* Was that a girl, boy? Man or woman? The face was so scary, without color. Without expression or distinction. She couldn't tell. The image blurred and then suddenly it wasn't there at all. The tingling sensation disappeared, too, leaving her empty and hollow and very confused.

Rhee's lids fluttered and she tried, she really did, to keep them open, but it was no good.

The vision wavered and she felt her knees buckle before she fell to the grass.

Chapter Two

Rhiannon heard the tinkling of bells and her mother's voice. She felt something poking and scratching against her cheek and her nostrils flared as she smelled...cow poop.

She opened her eyes, disoriented. Her mom helped her sit up, and Rhiannon blinked against the bright sunshine.

"Honey! Blessed be, I was so worried. What happened?"

Her mom's hand felt soft against her cheek. Rhiannon leaned into the touch and swallowed, which was hard to do since her mouth was so dry it felt like it had been caked with glue.

Her dad snapped his fingers and ran to the car. He returned with a half-empty bottle of spring water. "Here," he said as he unscrewed the lid and handed the bottle to her. "Are you all right?"

Rhiannon nodded as she gulped the water down. When the bottle was empty, she handed it back to her dad and wiped her mouth on her forearm.

Her mom babbled, "I turned around, and saw you fall, and you were staring at the house...what happened?"

Rhiannon wanted to know what happened too. How much of what she'd just experienced had been a psychic hallucination? Expressionless faces didn't stare out windows. It didn't make sense. It was entirely possible that the move had made her literally crazy. "Stop patting me, Mom. I'm fine, I just saw, uh..."

Ghost. Every freaky fiber of her being knew the image for what it was, she just didn't want to tell her parents about it. They'd spaz, and wanna move to Siberia or something. No, she wouldn't tell them until later, after she'd had a chance to be sure she'd really spotted her very first ghost. She didn't mask her thoughts quickly enough.

"A goat? You saw a goat in the attic window?" Her mom sat back on her heels, her bracelets jingling wildly.

Rhiannon was never more thankful that her mother's telepathic link was weak. She tried not to laugh as she glanced at her father.

He just looked confused. "I wonder what that means, a goat. Are you sure?"

Rhiannon nodded, deciding to go with it.

Starla beamed. "Why, that's a wonderful omen. Seeing a goat means that our fortunes will be improving! I knew this move was going to be good for us."

Rhiannon rolled her eyes and blew a breath from her nose. Her mom could find a portent in a garbage can.

"That's great, Rhee." Her dad cleared his throat and asked, "Feeling better? I can't believe the image was powerful enough for you to faint, you haven't done that since..."

She stood without assistance and put her hands on her hips to finish her dad's sentence. "Since you took me to Dr. Richards. He helped me, you know, more than you guys." All of her anger at her parents was back, just like that, as she remembered how they'd taken her away from her perfectly fine life.

"Can we go inside?" Rhee brushed off the seat of her pants, wondering what the bedroom she'd be sharing with a ghost...er...goat, looked like. Now that she wasn't in the middle of a psychic freak-out, she saw that the farmhouse was just like it had looked in the pictures. Neat and clean with a white front door and yellow trim.

"We should wait for the moving van," her dad said, looking down the gravel driveway with his hand shielding his eyes from the sun. "It should be here any minute, I wasn't driving *that* fast."

"I hope nothing is broken. I'll need my cleansing candles and my crystals. Just a quick run-through before we move the furniture in."

Her dad rocked back on his heels, agreeing with her mom's superstitions. *Let them believe in their dumb magick.* She knew the ghost was safe from her mother's purifying rituals. Dr. Richards said ghosts were merely imprints of those who had died traumatically, and they usually didn't even know that they were dead. And how could her mom sweep away what she couldn't even see?

"Well, can I go in at least?"

Her mom looked worried but her dad tossed her the keys. "Go ahead. The place has been empty for the past three months, so be careful of any six-foot dust bunnies."

Rhiannon snickered and tossed the keys back. "You know I don't need those, Dad."

He caught them and glared at her. "Normal kids do not unlock doors with their minds."

She shrugged, keeping her grin in place. "I keep telling you I'm a freak."

"Rhiannon! I absolutely do not want to hear that again, do you understand? You are our daughter, a gift from the moon

19

goddess. I—"

"Mom, here comes the moving van, I can hear it now. I'm just gonna go check out my room. Be right back, okay?"

Rhiannon didn't wait for any more arguments. She ran up the stairs to the porch as fast as she could. Anything but listen to the story of her sacred conception, *again.* Yuck.

She stood before the white door, thinking that this was maybe the coolest thing that had ever happened to her, like, *ever.* A ghost!

Yeah, it had scared her a little at first. She'd never seen a ghost before in her entire life, but now that she was getting used to the idea, she was pumped with excitement. Matthew and Tanya would be so jealous it was worth the shock, not that she'd tell them how scared she'd been. *No way.* Rhee would email her pals as soon as her dad had the internet up. Shuffling her feet, she realized she was stalling. But there wasn't anything to be afraid of. She was tough, everybody said so.

Rhiannon stared at the doorknob, willing it to be unlocked. She thought of the scary white face and hesitated. What was she supposed to do with the ghost once she found it? Could she just tell the thing to go to the light? Her heart raced and she muttered, "Don't be a chicken. Mrs. Edwards said that ghosts can't harm anyone." *And the medium would know.*

Narrowing her eyes, she concentrated on the lock and the handle. She heard the tumble and the click, and with a sigh of satisfaction she watched the knob turn and the door open in.

She wasn't prepared for the gust of cool air that greeted her, or the echo of laughter that was left like a memory.

Taking a step over the threshold, she called out, "Hello?" Rhiannon tensed as she waited for an answer. When none came, she giggled nervously. "What did you expect, a welcoming committee?" She shivered at the image of how incredibly freaky *that* would have been. A single ghost was one thing, right, but a houseful of them?

She exhaled and got her first real look at their new home. It was dark, mostly, since the lights were off and the windows closed with blinds. Using a simple flex of her mind, Rhee opened the curtains with a thought and a swift glance at them, then took a couple of steps into the living room. "Cool!"

The fireplace was huge, and took up almost an entire wall. The ceiling looked old-fashioned, with crisscrossed logs that you could tell were real trees, not that laminate wood stuff. *This might be okay*, she thought, *living here*. A haunted farmhouse! She wandered around downstairs, checking out the kitchen, the laundry area that had a door to the back yard, and a dining room that was open to the living area and the fireplace.

There was no sign of anything supernatural. "Man, this is old. I wonder if it would qualify for *Extreme Makeover: Home Edition*," she said in an awed whisper.

A thought came to her like an electric shock and she knew it wasn't from her mother.

"I hope you like my home."

The voice was feminine, had an English accent, and didn't belong in her head. Rhiannon froze with her hand on the banister leading upstairs and gulped. "Who are you?"

Faint laughter was the only answer she got, and it was somehow scarier than the eyeless image she'd seen at the attic window. Her hand shook. She was a fourteen-year-old girl who could make things move with her mind and do the occasional brain-meld. Dealing with a ghost could be exciting and new and great, but then again, maybe she'd wait to explore the upstairs until her parents came inside the house.

Her stomach was turning flip-flops and her mouth was as dry as the Painted Desert.

Matthew wouldn't be such a baby if he had the chance to see a ghost, he'd...what would he do? Rhee wasn't sure, but she doubted he'd be talking to himself. And Tanya, well, Tanya had more natural talent in her little finger than Rhiannon had with all her body parts combined. But then again, Tanya had never come face to, ugh, face with a real live ectoplasmic entity.

She was totally creeping herself out.

"There's nothing to be afraid of," the ghost said in a way that filled and stretched her whole mind.

"Get out of my head," Rhiannon demanded in a tone so small and shaky she didn't recognize her own voice.

"But I am so pleased to meet you, Rhiannon Godfrey."

She could feel goose bumps piling on top of goose bumps and the hair against her scalp prickled. "What do you want?"

"Come upstairs and I'll show you."

She felt the tug at her hands and she gripped the banister tighter. Her blood was ice in her veins and she couldn't move a muscle. "Go away."

The sound of laughter, somehow sad and lonely, raced through the air and bounced off the walls. *"I cannot. Do you think I've not tried? You are the first person to talk to me in many years, Rhiannon."*

Oh man, oh man, this is horrible, we never should have moved here. The hairs on her arms were standing straight up and she was going to faint again if she didn't get out of this house. *Now.* She was *so* unprepared for this!

She broke away from the railing, using every ounce of her psychic willpower, her eyes darting around the room looking for visible evidence. There was none. "Leave me alone," she warned.

A torrent of cold flew around her like a windstorm.

"Don't go!" The young female ghost's voice had a pleading

quality that reached past the fear to Rhee's heart.

It was enough of an opening that Rhiannon was once again rooted to the spot, terrified by the despair that enveloped her. She couldn't run, she couldn't scream, she couldn't move. She, Rhiannon Godfrey, the girl prodigy who toured and lectured on how to move things with your mind, couldn't *think*. Then the air stilled as if someone had flipped a switch and she realized she might have bitten off more than she could chew.

What was her problem? She wasn't a trained medium, she was just a weird kid who could do some psychic tricks. Sending a ghost to the stars was a little out of her league. *There.* She'd admitted her failings. Now could she go?

Another wave of loneliness washed over her like rain. Rhee was powerless to budge from the stairs, and yet she knew she had to get outside! She desperately had to re-group.

The voice inside her head whispered, *"But, Rhiannon, I've been waiting for you."*

Chapter Three

Rhiannon closed her eyes tight and concentrated really hard in order to break free of the ghost's psychic hold, then sprinted for the front door. It slammed shut in front of her, but she yanked it back open with both hands and tripped, literally, out onto the porch.

No way, she thought, *no way am I living here. I obviously am not up to dealing with a ghost, no matter how easy I thought it would be. It's too much.*

Beads of sweat stood out on her forehead and she was breathing like she'd run a thirty-second mile. She shielded her eyes against the glaring sun. She wanted to go home!

"Rhiannon! Honey, come meet our neighbor; his family lives down the road and he's brought us a *cow.*"

Her mother's tinkling voice was hostess perfect. Rhiannon glanced out at the driveway and noticed that the moving van had arrived, blocking the Godfreys' car from view. Two burly guys were unloading boxes, probably trying to find her mom's candles first. She saw her dad grinning, her mom was smiling and...

No fair, she thought with a sinking jolt. The neighbor was *hot.* And here she was dressed in cuffed jeans, a ratty T-shirt and sneakers that her mom kept trying to throw away.

Rhiannon brushed her long, red hair out of her eyes with one hand and wiped the other on her thigh. She'd just battled a talking ghost and now she had to switch to a social situation, which wasn't exactly her strong point. Especially with a guy too cute for words. She finally managed a totally stupid question. "A cow?"

Her mom laughed. "It seems that the Roberts family has been holding on to her for us. The other family left her here when they moved, so poor Betsy was out loose in the woods until she got hungry enough to find the Roberts' petunias. I'll have to make her some burdock water to help her get over her fear of betrayal, with a few rose petals added so that she'll know she's safe here with us. Home."

The hot neighbor guy's eyebrows arched.

Rhiannon swallowed from her safe place on the porch. She didn't have any make-up on, no jewelry, and she hadn't run a comb through her hair since morning. And to top it all off, her mom was spouting herbal potions as if she were still practicing the craft in Vegas.

Dread filled her from head to toe. She would rather go back inside and face the ghost than meet the gorgeous hick with the cow. He was going to hate her, eventually. Almost everybody did once they found out she was a freakazoid.

His hair peeked dark blond beneath his cowboy hat. He wore his black T-shirt tucked into his worn jeans, and his scuffed cowboy boots looked perfectly comfortable. He tossed her a smile that made her sensitive psyche jump. "Hey," he called.

Rhiannon slowly went down the porch stairs, feeling like an idiot for being caught staring. Well, she thought, he was so cute he was probably used to it. She stopped in front of him and nodded once. "Hi. I'm Rhiannon."

"Great name. I'm Jared."

Her mom lifted one hand in a harried gesture. "Jared, what lovely manners you have. I should have introduced us, but instead I just was so surprised by the *cow*. Well, this is Miles, Rhee's dad, and I'm Starla. Did you know that Rhiannon comes from the Celtic—?"

"Mom!" Rhiannon closed her eyes wondering if and when her mother would stop embarrassing her.

Like, never.

One of the moving guys dropped a box and a tinkling crash sounded. Her mom's eyes opened wide and she grabbed Miles by the hand. "That better not have been my crystals...you bought insurance, right?" Rhee saw the little frown right above her mom's nose—a sure sign of worry—as her parents disappeared around the giant van.

Rhiannon was left alone with Jared. Would he roll his eyes or make a smart-aleck comment about her parents?

The cow mooed, but Jared said nothing. His gaze was friendly and relaxed.

"Uh..." She stammered, then blushed, her pale skin burning with discomfort. She was so not cool in these situations. "Betsy?"

Jared grinned, scratching the black-and-white cow behind the ears. "Kinda dumb name, compared to yours, but she's a good animal."

Rhiannon watched the cow blink large, ink black eyes. "If she were a cat, she'd be purring," she said.

"You have a cat?"

His voice was deeper than Matthew's. He was taller too. Or maybe it was just the hat. "Oh, uh, *no*. I've never had a pet."

He smiled, showing white teeth that seemed even whiter

against his tanned skin. He could be a walking advertisement for a "Drink Milk" commercial, she thought.

"You should get a barn cat, they eat the mice. My cat is due to have a litter any day now."

A kitten? Who ate mice? *Ew.* She was saved from answering when Betsy stepped forward as daintily as a princess with hooves and nipped her T-shirt with big yellow teeth. Nervous of anything bigger than she was, Rhiannon stepped back, pulling her clothes with her. "Bad cow," she told it.

Jared laughed. "Your shirt's green. Maybe she's hungry. If the pen is fixed you could take her there."

Rhiannon scrunched her nose. "Like I would know? We just got here." She eyed the cow, and the cow eyed her. "Besides, I think she likes you. Maybe you could take her back to your house."

Jared tilted up the brim of his hat and said, "Well, Betsy ate all of my mom's petunias. Which is why when we drove by and saw your car here, Mom sent me with the cow. It was return Betsy or send her to the butcher."

"The butcher?" Was he serious? An urge to protect the poor cow from being made into hamburger had her jerking the rope from Jared's hand.

He looked surprised. "Hey, I was just kidding. We wouldn't kill somebody else's cow."

Rhiannon felt the blush heat up her face. "Oh." Why did she always have to make a fool of herself? She kept the rope in her hand and relied on sarcasm to cover her humiliation. "How nice. You just kill your own."

He shrugged. "That's what cows are for, if they aren't dairy. So, are you going to Crystal Lake High?"

Why did he have to be so hot and then turn out to be a

carnivore? Oh well, she mused. It was good to know he wasn't perfect. Finding a flaw made it easier to look at him. His eyes were new-mown-grass green and curious.

Rhee swallowed, knowing she had zero business checking out his eyes. "Well, I don't think so, I mean, I want to be—"

"Yes!" her mom interrupted from behind her. "She'll be in ninth grade. What about you?"

Jared turned to her parents, who were obviously done checking on the moving guys, and answered, "Yes, ma'am. My sister and I will both be freshmen this year."

Starla clapped her hands and Rhiannon's grasp on Betsy's rope tightened. "Twins! How auspicious. Are you a Gemini?"

Her dad put his hand on her mom's shoulder. "Honey, I think we can start moving in the box you wanted." His voice held a tone of warning and Rhiannon was grateful that at least one parent was trying to blend.

Her mom pursed her lips, obviously not taking the hint, so her dad jumped in with a direct question to Jared. "We've never had a cow; is there anything we need to know?"

Jared's confused expression made Rhiannon smile.

"Uh, well, sir. She's not a dairy cow or anything, so feed and water, until you decide when to butcher her." Jared patted Betsy's belly. "She's healthy. Lots of steak in there."

Jared laughed but stopped when he noticed the horrified looks on her parents' faces. Rhiannon was sure that hers appeared just as grossed out. She felt kinda bad for him though, as she watched him shuffle his feet uncomfortably.

He said, "I should probably be getting back home."

Rhiannon decided to take pity on him and chimed in with an explanation. "We're vegetarians. No meat."

Now it was his turn to look horrified. "Oh. Okay. Sorry."

Did he have to be so cute?

Her dad hid a smile behind his fisted hand. "Nothing to be sorry about. Listen, before you go, would you mind tying Betsy to the fence? And if you could let Rhiannon know what to do with her until we can find her another home, I'd appreciate it. Thank you, Jared." Her father stuck out his hand and Jared shook it.

He sure is polite.

Her mom touched the citrine amulet that hung from her neck. "Many blessings upon you and your family. We thank you."

Rhiannon winced, but Jared looked startled and mumbled, "You're welcome."

She pulled on the rope before her mom could say anything else too revealing. "C'mon, Betsy. Let's go figure out where you'll be living."

"Yank harder, otherwise she won't go," Jared advised as he practically walked on her heels. *To get away from her strange parents?* She couldn't exactly blame him, not when she thought they were plenty weird too.

"But I don't want to hurt her." Rhiannon wondered if she and Betsy could mind-meld once the cowboy left.

He laughed and kicked a pebble with his boot. "You won't. Cows are stubborn but stupid. She won't bite you unless you put your hand in her mouth."

Rhiannon bristled. Had he just called her cow stupid? Looks were *so* not everything. "I'll make sure to keep my fingers to myself."

"Here, let me tie her for you. I've actually gotten pretty good at this. Betsy seems to have a knack for getting loose."

Rhiannon handed him the rope and watched how

competent his hands were as he tied the knot around the fence. She'd have managed to get her fingers stuck in the rope, she knew it. "Nice job...does Betsy's wandering have anything to do with a petunia addiction?"

He laughed and Rhee sucked in a breath, deciding then and there to forgive him for being a know-it-all since he was just so gorgeous. Like, *People Magazine's* "Most Beautiful People"-cover gorgeous. And the meat eating thing...well, it wasn't like she was going out with him. *Too bad.*

He was still grinning at her. "I don't think she'll need rehab."

Rhee smiled back, wondering if this was flirting. "I'm sorry about your mom's flowers."

"It's all right. She'll buy more. Well," he said as he slowly backed away from her without breaking eye contact, "I guess I'll see ya around."

Rhiannon's nerves danced in anticipation. "Uh, okay." Why couldn't she think of anything funny or interesting to say? She would come up with tons of stuff, later, when he was long gone. Sheesh, she was such a dweeb.

He stuck his hands in his jeans. "I've never heard of giving a cow rose petals before."

Rhiannon averted her eyes. "Well, my mom, she's really into natural stuff."

"Oh. Like New Age?"

She chewed her lower lip. "Sort of like that." She could see him trying to figure everything out. And, she knew from past experience, once he did, he wouldn't be so cool. Dr. Richards said it was human nature to hate what you didn't understand.

He dipped his chin and said, "Bye, then."

She waved, quickly turning her back so that she was facing

Betsy. Her eyes filled with angry tears. *Make new friends,* her mom said. Like it was as easy as snapping your fingers. Having to deal with psychic abilities was hard enough when it came to meeting new people. And when you added in the fact that her mom was a witch...she didn't have a chance for normal.

Chapter Four

Rhiannon stood outside with Betsy for as long as she could. Thinking about Jared was cool, but she didn't want to think about his sister, or making new friends at school. "I am *so* stalling. I have to go in there and face what is in that house sooner or later, Betsy."

She took the time to consider the ghost who lived in her bedroom. According to Mrs. Edwards, there was no way that it could hurt her. But ghosts weren't supposed to be able to talk like regular people, either. And while she'd heard the voice plain as day, she hadn't seen a thing.

It wasn't like she could ask her parents for a different room, not after she'd made such a fuss about wanting the attic for herself. She'd wanted privacy, she said, and didn't they owe her for making her move? The fact that it had a skylight was frosting on the cake. She'd been looking forward to putting her bed beneath the glass so that she could stare out at the stars before falling asleep.

She hadn't counted on anything creepy staring back at her.

The cow nudged her. Rhiannon cautiously reached out to scratch Betsy behind the ears, just as she'd seen Jared do. "You like that? What a good girl, Betsy. Don't worry. You'll be happy here. No butcher, no rendering plant. I'll even make sure you have all the petunias you could ever eat."

Betsy snuffled and blinked her dark eyes.

"You aren't stupid at all, are ya?" Rhee sent out a psychic probe, but didn't get a connection. She'd just have to communicate the old-fashioned way. Speech.

The cow's tail twitched as she swatted a fly off her back.

"I didn't think so. Wanna tell me what I should do? I figure I can tell my folks about the ghost and my mom can get all excited, in a bad way, and move us out of the farm. The bad part about that is we won't go back to Vegas, not after what happened. She'll probably set us up in the mountains if this doesn't work out. Instead of country hicks, I can learn how to get along with the hillbillies."

Betsy laid back her ears.

Sighing, Rhiannon continued laying her problems out to Betsy. "So, if I don't tell Mom about the ghost, then I can stay here and solve its problem on my own, which could get me back to Vegas. I'm not usually such a baby. I was surprised, that's all." Rhiannon braced herself to go inside.

Betsy shook her head. Or maybe she was just trying to get rid of the bug by her muzzle.

Rhiannon looked up at the attic window. Nothing. The space was empty, the window unbroken and clean. She narrowed her eyes, thinking out loud, "This could be very cool, right? I mean, I can't be afraid, because I want to be a parapsychologist, just like Dr. Richards. And if I can prove to everybody that I have the power to send ghosts back to the beyond, well...Mom and Dad will have to see that I'm serious about going back to the institute. That whole Maddie thing was an accident."

Betsy mooed in disbelief.

"It was!"

"Rhiannon? Come on in, honey. Help us with the boxes."

She stayed by the fence a moment longer, gathering her courage. Rhee sorta wished that her mom's cleansing rituals would clear the ghost, but she doubted it. Maybe she'd snag a crystal just in case. It couldn't hurt to have the Goddess on your side when you were dealing with the eerie and strange, just in case she couldn't find a scientific reason for what was happening.

"Wish me luck, Betsy, here I go."

The cow swished her tail and batted her eyelashes while Rhiannon took the first steps toward the house.

"Be brave and strong. *Show no fear.*" She repeated the phrase until she got to the porch steps.

Her mother came to the door, a candle in her hand and a shocked look on her face. "You crave a beer?"

Rhiannon stumbled on the first step. "What? Mom, I swear that you get worse at reading my mind the older I get."

"What were you really thinking?"

She paused and crossed her arms over her chest. Brave, no fear. A beer? Her mom was seriously losin' it. She said, "I don't know." Subject change, quick. "Jared seems okay."

Her mom smiled, brushing her long, wavy red hair away from her face. "Yes, he was a very handsome young man." Her smile faded and her eyes narrowed. "You'd better not be drinking, Rhiannon Selene Godfrey. Now, come help bring the boxes up to your room. We have to paint it, so put them in the center. We'll pick out carpet and curtains...silver, white, and blue, the colors of the Moon Goddess. It will be beautiful!"

"Hey, did you already go up there? I haven't even had a chance to see it yet." Had her mom scared away the ghost, just when she'd decided to face it?

Her mom waved the hand that wasn't holding the lavender scented candle. "No, no. I wanted to get the downstairs cleansed first. So don't start putting things away, yet. We'll set up your furniture tomorrow, after we finish painting."

Rhiannon ran to the stairs leading up to her room. Now that she'd made her decision regarding the ghost, she didn't want to wait.

What if she wasn't dealing with the average ghost?

Don't think that, she said to herself.

"A pink hat? I don't remember you having a pink hat, honey. But it'll turn up in one of these boxes. Don't worry."

Rhiannon shook her head and continued up the stairs. "Thanks, Mom."

She reached the second floor and stopped. Every wall in the house had been painted stark white, and the super-thin hallway leading up to the attic was no exception.

The skinny door at the top had an old-fashioned oval-shaped brass knob, like from the old movies she liked to watch late at night.

The ones where the ditzy big-boobed blonde always goes into the dark room and you know she's gonna end up bitten by a vampire or something.

"Okay. Maybe I shouldn't barge in there." Her stomach tightened. She felt like she was on the very top of the roller coaster and she was just about to drop.

She prepared herself by putting up her mental "force shields", as Dr. Richards liked to call them. He'd explained that visualizing an invisible layer of energy would help her to block out unwanted psychic experiences. "It would be good if I'd been able to finish my training," she muttered. Dang her parents.

Nevertheless, she gave it her best shot. She paused, bowed

her head and imagined herself safe inside a bubble, untouchable.

She took a deep breath and walked up the rest of the stairs.

Just before the door was a small square wooden floor space with barely enough room to turn around on. There was a single naked bulb hanging from the ceiling with a rusted chain pull dangling and decorated with cobwebs.

"I take it this room hasn't been used much." Her voice echoed around her in the space and she shivered. She made herself reach for the small brass door handle, actually stalling for time by opening it with her hand. Maybe it wouldn't open. It looked like the kind of door that would need a key. She swallowed. A *skeleton* key.

When had she turned into such a wimp?

She exhaled, pulled her hand back and wiped both sweaty palms on her jeans. "Okay, here we go."

She felt the cool brass knob beneath her fingers and twisted it, opening the door slowly. The old hinges creaked as if the door hadn't been opened in hundreds of years.

"Ridiculous," she muttered. She knew for sure that the skylight had been installed twenty years ago; that fact had been on the realtor's little fact sheet she'd peeked at.

And twenty years wasn't that long. She felt along the inside wall for a light switch. She found it and flipped it up. The depressing shadowy grayness was suddenly bright. Peering inside, she saw nothing too odd and stepped over the raised threshold. She was in. Her room. The one she shared with a ghost.

Oh yeah, she thought with a shiver, *this is completely beyond anything I've ever experienced before.* Ghosts. Entities that were bound in a tragic experience at the time of their death, doomed to replay the same incident over and over, like a skipping CD.

Her ghost didn't seem to fit that category.

What if it was something more?

Rhee was surprised at how dark the room was; she'd been expecting it be bright because of the skylight. She looked up at the pane of glass inset into the ceiling and noticed it was caked over with dirt and mud. "Looks like someone was allergic to soap."

She let her guard down slowly, inch by inch, until she was certain she was alone in her room. Empty of all energy forces, except for her own.

"Fess up, Rhee. You're a little disappointed." Her voice echoed back at her in the mostly empty attic space. *Maybe*, she admitted. She'd had herself all geared up for a confrontation that hadn't happened.

She took the opportunity to check out her room, which ran the length of the entire house. The walls were filthy, and cobwebs looked like dirty yarn as they ran from corner to corner.

Had this room always been neglected? It couldn't have been. No one would have bothered to install the skylight if it was just used for storage. So why had they let it go to ruin?

She forgot all about the state of filth when she realized that a portion of the room was behind a floor-to-ceiling partition. Just looking at the small entryway and the deep dark shadows behind the partial wall gave her the willies.

Bad, bad, bad. That hidden corner was bad. She knew it with every extrasensory perception she had.

Rhee felt her eyes widen as she was smacked with a sense of danger. The wallop of sudden fear was paralyzing and completely different from how she'd felt earlier. This was wrong. She was being invaded from the toes up, turned to ice like in an X-Men movie, her body was going numb, part by part.

Could the coldness kill her? She struggled and put up her shields. "What the heck?" Cool sweat dribbled down her back and she had an idea that she was dealing with something other than *her* ghost. Now that she had something to compare it to, Rhee realized that her earlier scare came from not understanding what was going on, while this...she struggled and squirmed. This was *bad.*

She fought the cold by imagining healing warmth and was finally able to back away from the partition until her shoulders hit the attic door. Rhiannon couldn't take her eyes off of the corner. Not when she was feeling like something might, possibly, definitely, jump out of the dark and attack her.

This wasn't a puny scare, this was closer to nail-biting terror. The kind where a malevolent force is waiting to catch you, skin you alive and eat you.

She shivered and stared at the darkness.

Her hands trembled and it seemed as if the force was getting stronger, compelling her to go to the corner, into the dark recesses of the attic. *"Come, come"*, something was calling to her, and to her horror, she saw herself take a step forward on the splintered wooden floor.

"No!" she yelled, struggling against the evil web that was drawing her in.

A cool push of air instantly severed the connection and Rhiannon stumbled back just as her mom threw open the door to her bedroom, knocking Rhee to the floor.

"By the Goddess, Rhiannon! You can't stay here!"

Chapter Five

They ate dinner that night standing over a cluttered counter filled with unpacked boxes, partially empty crates, and lots of candles. Rhiannon swallowed the last bite of her veggie burger, then wiped the ketchup from her mouth with a napkin.

"I don't want to sleep in the spare bedroom," she complained again. More to keep in practice than because she actually wanted to sleep in the attic.

Which she didn't. *No way, José.* Not until the room had been fumigated, evil-bombed and cleansed. Three times. She had never been happier to see her mother, who had taken one look at the garbage in the attic and declared it uninhabitable for man or beast.

"I still say I heard you calling for me." Starla arched a red brow.

"I didn't, Mom. I swear."

"Don't swear. And it came through so clear...you were scared."

Rhiannon squirmed. She had not called for her mother, not once while she was in the attic. "I told you that your telepathy is whacked."

She wasn't telling her mom about the corner. And she sure wasn't sleeping up there until whatever had been there was beyond gone.

Rhiannon had learned a long time ago that things weren't always what they seemed, but Dr. Richards had helped explain the unusual with scientific facts. She bit her thumbnail and wondered what he'd say about the thing in the dark.

"Is the computer up at least?" She really wanted to talk to Tanya and Matthew. Bad.

Her dad wadded up his one-hundred percent recyclable paper plate. "Of course. How can I keep my clients if I'm not online?" He winked at her and Rhiannon decided to cut her folks some slack. They loved her, and she knew it.

She loved them too. Not that she was gonna tell them right away. There could still be some benefit in playing the angry, you-owe-me teen.

She kissed his cheek. "Thanks, Dad. I should've realized that an internet junkie would need his fix right away."

Her mom smiled. "Why don't you see if Tanya and Matthew are online? They might hurt themselves laughing when you tell them about your new cow."

"We aren't keeping her," her dad announced.

"Yes, we are!" Rhiannon and her mom answered in unison.

Hanging his head, he mumbled, "I was afraid this would happen. You've already bonded with her. What are we going to do with a cow?"

Rhiannon swept crumbs off the counter and into the garbage. "I've never had a pet. So long as I don't have to pick up cow poop, I'm all for feeding her and stuff."

She put her arm around her mom. "Please?"

Her mom sniffed. "Pets are normal things, Miles. I think we should keep her. Besides, if we give Betsy to anyone else, they might *eat* her. I just couldn't live with myself, honey."

"Fine. But a normal pet is a cat or a dog. Maybe a goldfish, Starla. Not a cow."

Her mom crossed her arms, sending her bracelets jingling like wind chimes. "I'm doing the best I can, dear. Go on, Rhiannon, go see what Tanya and Matthew are up to."

As she walked by her mom added, "Make sure you tell Tanya about how gorgeous Jared is. It's time you got over that crush you had on Matthew."

"Mo-om." Did her mom have to notice every little thing?

The computer was set up in the living room, next to the gigantic fireplace. Her mom had stuck candles in the four corners of the room honoring the north, south, east, and west and the elements attached to each. Earth, fire, air, and water. And in the center of the room was a discrete (for her mother, anyway) altar dedicated to the Goddess.

A white candle for purity was lit and burning cheerfully. Next to the computer her mom had placed a vase of wildflowers she'd picked. To prod the creative mind, she'd said.

Her dad had grumbled that he dealt with taxes that were already creative enough.

She logged on under her own screen name, Psycho Babble.

"Yes!" she said under breath. Tanya and Matthew were both on Instant Messaging.

Her fingers flew over the keyboard.

Rhiannon: *Hey. Made it to No Where. Cool farmhouse. Miss you*

Tanya: *Miss u 2*

Matthew: *You've only been gone a day. I'll miss you tomorrow*

Rhiannon grinned. Man, did she miss her friends.

Rhiannon: *Hey, guys, got a secret. Promise not to tell?*

Tanya: *Duh!*

Matthew: *Maybe*

Rhiannon: *I'm not sharing until you promise, Mattster*

She tapped her fingers on the desk as she waited for him to make up his mind. He was messing with her, like always.

Matthew: *K*

Now that it was time to share her secret, she wasn't sure how to say it.

Tanya: *What r u waiting 4? I know it's not x-mas*

Rhiannon chuckled. Wiccans didn't celebrate Christmas, but they did celebrate Yuletide, which was around the Winter Solstice and in December too.

Rhiannon: *The farm is haunted*

Tanya: *R u sure? Cool!*

Matthew: *Do you want me to tell the doc?*

Rhiannon: *No! You promised. I can handle it*

Then she typed all that had happened since her arrival earlier that day, including the malignant force that seemed to live in the corner of the attic.

Tanya: *Not good, u could be hurt*

Rhee held her breath, waiting for Matthew to answer. He was sixteen and gorgeous, genius-smart, and not interested in her other than in a little-sister way. Rhiannon found herself counting on his intelligence.

Matthew: *Sounds like a spirit, not ghost. A discarnate entity that has an attachment to the house. Since she said your name, she could have formed an attachment to you*

Rhiannon sat back in her chair, crossing her legs beneath her.

Rhiannon: *Like in that movie Poltergeist? Where the cute blonde girl gets sucked into the closet?*

Tanya: *2 funny. I loved that movie*

Matthew: *Stop messing around, this isn't a joke*

She could picture both of her friends just by the way they typed. Tanya would be listening to grunge music and watching her lava lamp ooze while Matthew would be chewing the end of a pencil and frowning while he concentrated.

Matthew got so irritated when she and Tanya didn't take their abilities seriously. Probably because other than the fire-starting thing, he was kind of a psychic dud, but a whiz with the high-tech equipment. Plus, he had a save-the-world complex, which was nice, but didn't leave room for crushes.

Matthew: *Hey!!! U there?*

She got back to the present with a sigh.

Rhiannon: *Sorry. What else can you tell me? I want to handle this myself. My parents will have to let me go back to the institute if I can save a ghost from eternal purgatory*

Tanya: *Give the Dairy Cow Parade a chance, Rhee baby. I got 2 go—be careful!*

Rhiannon: *C ya*

Matthew: *Let me do some more research, I'll get back to you. Has the spirit shown herself to you, or given you her name?*

Rhee thought of the image at the attic window. Had that been the same ghost who had talked to her? Or something completely different? It would be better to wait and find out before freaking Matthew out even more.

Rhiannon: *No name. But don't say anything, not even to Mrs. Edwards. I really want to do this myself*

Matthew: *I don't think you can do it alone*

Rhiannon inhaled through her nose, hurt and angry that her friend didn't believe in her. Make that *ex*-friend.

She logged off without saying good-bye.

Her mom peeked around the corner. "So. How are they doing?"

"Tanya's great." *Matthew's a jerk*, she thought.

"Matthew found work?"

"Uh, no. Geez, Mom. Matthew, uh, he's just busy, that's all."

"Mmm. Well, I'm glad you got to talk to them both. And there's always the telephone. That little gadget that rings? So you can hear the person you're talking to?"

Her mom laughed at her own joke and Rhiannon couldn't help but giggle. Her mom was so full of high-spirited energy.

Spirits. Man, she was so mad at Matthew. Would he blab her secrets? Maybe she wouldn't talk to him, ever. She'd just erase him from her email and that would be the end of that.

"Rhiannon, are you okay?"

She looked up. "Yeah. Great. I'm tired."

Her mom handed her a cup of chamomile tea. "It's been a hard day. Emotionally as well as physically. Are you really disappointed about not being able to sleep in your room? I can't believe the mess it's in. Shameful."

Rhiannon hooked her right leg under her butt and swung the left one back and forth. "Not really. The spare bedroom will be fine. It makes more sense to wait until the attic is ready."

And empty.

"More tea?"

Startled, Rhiannon looked down at her half-full mug. "No!" She was going to have to do a better job at blocking her mom, and whoever else might want to pick her brain. She must be more tired than she thought if Starla was able to pick up random stuff going through her head.

"Well, maybe you should hit the hay, then. We've got shopping to do tomorrow. Three weeks until you're a high-schooler! I didn't see any sign of a mall. I wonder if the grocery store will have a decent organic food section." Her mom sat back on the couch, her own mug of tea in her hands. "A farmer's market—I betcha they'll have one every Saturday around here."

Rhiannon noticed the dreamy expression on her mom's face and couldn't help but say, "I can't believe you are so happy."

"Why wouldn't I be? I have been blessed in so many ways. I love this house. I can feel its historic aura. And I think you will be given the opportunity to finally have a regular childhood." Her mom held up a hand. "Not that you're a baby, but still...to go to the prom, and the movies, to have sleepovers and homework."

Her mom sipped from her mug. "This will be wonderful for you, Rhiannon, so why shouldn't I be happy?"

Guilt weighted her to the chair. Her parents had had friends and jobs in Las Vegas that they'd given up because of her.

Her mom had owned a supply store for Wiccans and witches, and her dad was an accountant for some major companies. Luckily he'd been able to work out most of his accounts online, and for one week a month he'd get to go back to Vegas.

She wanted to go back too. Why couldn't they see that this normal childhood that they wanted so badly for her wasn't in the cards?

Rhiannon got up before she started bawling. "Thanks, Mom. Is the bed already made? I'm beat."

"Of course. I put a few of your things in the room too. Just because it is temporary doesn't mean you shouldn't have some of your stuff around, right?"

Rhiannon smiled, even though she didn't feel like it. "Yeah."

She put her mug in the sink and walked up to the second floor. Guilt, guilt, guilt echoed with every heavy step she took.

If only Maddie hadn't moved into their apartment building. If only Maddie hadn't been such a...

If only Maddie hadn't had such a big mouth, she thought as she crawled beneath the covers of her temporary bed.

She used her mind to shut off the light.

But the memory of what she'd done stayed front and center until she finally fell into a fitful sleep.

It *hadn't* been her fault.

Chapter Six

Rhiannon was bored out of her ever-loving mind.

This was summer in the country and it sucked. Big time. *Sure,* she thought, *me and Betsy have bonded. But Mom is so busy cleaning and painting, and somehow everyone is staying clear of the attic, and Dad...*she dropped her head to her arms and stared out the window toward the barn.

Her dad had painted the old barn white with red trim, and Betsy followed him around like a dog. *Traitor.*

It had been the longest week of her life. To add torture on top of injustice, the morning storm had knocked out both the TV *and* the internet.

She sighed, lifted her head and glanced toward the kitchen. She'd already gone through an entire bag of Doritos that her mom didn't know about, along with a Snickers bar. She'd had two sodas and it wasn't even lunchtime yet.

What was she going to do with her day? If she kept eating she'd be fat and zit-faced for the first day of school. Just what she needed to fit in with everyone else.

"Hi," she imagined saying. "I'm Rhiannon, the freaky geek with the zit on her cheek."

She walked over to the couch and threw herself down on the plump cushions.

Tanya was in England for the institute, and Matthew was on her *Do Not Talk To* list. She was almost starting to wish her ghost would appear, just so she'd have something to do. But the ghost was a no-show, and Rhiannon was beginning to wonder if she'd imagined the entire thing.

"Rhiannon!" Her mom's voice floated down the stairs. "Honey, let's get up in that attic. Come and help me, this is your room, after all. Where has the week gone? I can't believe we haven't gotten to it yet."

Rhiannon sat up reluctantly. *And I can't believe that I'm excited about cleaning my room,* she thought.

"Bringing a broom? Good idea, honey. I've got the rest of the cleaning supplies up here already."

Rhiannon shook her head, grabbed the broom and dustpan, and headed up the stairs. "Wow! What's that smell? It's nice."

Her mom radiated happiness. "Thank you, Rhee! I found wild lavender at the edge of the little forest, that I've brought inside to dry. Time is just flying by, and I know I should probably be inside more, getting things done, but I'd forgotten how wonderful it is to commune with nature. I find myself outside, just breathing in the fresh air. It's divine. Why haven't you said anything about the attic?"

Rhiannon searched her mom's face, wondering if she knew about the ghost, then she shrugged. No way. Her mom couldn't keep a secret like that. "I dunno. I've been busy." Ha, busy researching ghost stuff on the internet, but coming up empty. Most of the sites were filled with wackos and dumb stories that were so not true.

She hadn't felt anything creepy or scary since the first day they'd arrived. No girl ghost-voice, no faces, no cold numbness. But then again, the lingering fear of the corner partition had kept her away from upstairs. She paused at the landing and looked up toward the attic door. She preferred to think of the past week as one of strategic research, not cowardice.

Calling herself a baby, she sent out mental feelers to the room. She didn't come up with anything at all. Maybe whatever it was had actually left during her mom's cleansing ritual.

But how could her mom's magickal prayers, which were nothing more than wishful thinking, have more power than her psychic abilities, which were explainable science?

Too mind-boggling a question for such a lazy day. Rhiannon followed her mom up the narrow stairs to her room. The dangling light bulb had been replaced with an old-fashioned light fixture. "Where'd we get that?"

"Your dad found it in the barn. He's come across a lot of old stuff. You might have fun going through some of it."

Her mom opened the door and Rhiannon braced herself for negative energy.

None came. The room was empty. Had she imagined everything?

She walked all the way in and glanced at the partition separating the back part of the attic from the rest of the room.

A remnant of fear made her shiver, but she couldn't let the memory overpower her common sense. She *so* didn't believe in the boogie man. When she was younger, Dr. Richards had shown her countless books explaining why things went 'bump' in the night. A scientist searched for, and usually found, a logical answer to other people's hysteria.

Logic and reason. If there was something evil here, it would be up to her to banish it. Rhiannon looked around the room with growing interest. Light was everywhere, dispelling the remaining scariness like smoke. "Did Dad clean the skylight?"

"He sure did. I was a little worried when he was on the roof, but he managed."

Her mom always sounded proud of Dad's accomplishments. "Not bad for a guy who couldn't change a light bulb," Rhiannon said, kinda proud too. "Next thing you know he's going to want a riding lawn mower."

"Wouldn't surprise me. Okay, I have the paint, but we really need to empty out that storage space over there—" her mom pointed to the dark corner, "—and then it's a matter of scrubbing and elbow grease."

Thanks to the clean skylight, the corner looked innocent, but an unexpected chill raced across her shoulders just the same. *So much for logic and reason.* "Did you do the cleansing ritual with candles?"

"Yes, I was going to use the smudging technique using fresh herbs, but I don't think we need it. Do you?"

Rhiannon shook her head, "Nah." But she stored away that last piece of information in case she had to do it herself later. If she could. She hadn't worked a spell since she was like, what, seven? "Let's leave the worst part of the room for last, Mom."

Dr. Richards had taught her how to protect herself from unwanted psychic intrusions, which was the equivalent of mental eavesdropping, and had zippo to do with blocking evil entities. What could she do to protect herself? Resorting to magick might have to become an option. The idea held a secret thrill.

Peering at the partition, her mom rubbed her arms as if she'd caught a draft, and then she walked to the window on the opposite side of the room and stood in the direct sunlight. "All right," she agreed. "This is the bigger portion, anyway."

It took them three hours of working side by side, but when they were finished the room was spotless and shiny and ready to be painted.

Sitting back on her heels, her mom wiped her forehead. "Whew! Well, Rhee, I like it. I wasn't sure about this at first, but now..." Her mom surveyed the room with a perfectionist's eyes. "It's clean."

Rhiannon laughed. "You forgot about behind the partition."

Her mom frowned. "No, I didn't. Why don't you get started on that while I go get us some lemonade? That space is small— maybe Dad could turn it into a closet for you?" She got to her feet and walked to the partial wall. "I wonder... I would be willing to bet that it used to be one."

Rhiannon followed her mom across the room. A closet? That made sense. But it didn't feel right.

"All this needs is a bright lamp, some paint, and some new shelves. Those look too rickety. Oh, Rhee, I think it will be wonderful!"

Rhiannon swallowed. The interior of the partial wall was cut off from all the light that bathed the rest of the room. Leaving the corner very dark. "I'll need to get a light from downstairs."

"Take the one from your nightstand. My goodness, just look at all of these boxes. What could be in here?"

Secrets. *Rows and rows of secrets.*

"Arrows and sneakers? Do you think so?" Her mom looked doubtful. "You stay here. I'll get the lamp and the lemonade."

Starla left and the back of Rhiannon's neck immediately prickled. She looked around the room and watched the air shimmer and thicken. She paused, then relaxed as she realized she wasn't the least bit frightened. It was the return of the first ghost. "Where have you been?"

The young woman's voice said softly, "Resting. Do you

think it is easy making oneself heard?"

Rhiannon licked her dry lips and stepped away from the corner. "I, um, I guess not. What's your name?"

"Suzanne."

"How old are you?"

"Much older than you." Laughter echoed, full of sunshine.

"You don't sound like an old woman." Rhee remembered Matthew's concern over getting too close with the spirit, but brushed it aside to satisfy her own curiosity. "Are you a teenager, I mean, *were* you?" Oops, she thought with a twinge of guilt. What if Suzanne didn't realize she'd passed on?

"I was a woman, but now I am dead, Rhiannon. I know this."

"Well, don't you think you need to hit the light, or something?"

"What does that mean? I cannot leave my home."

"But there is a better life. Summerland, Heaven, reincarnation, whatever you believe, it has to be better than wandering the same old house for...how long?"

A cool breeze swept over her skin. "I don't know in years. I have seen many families come and go. But no one could hear me before you. I am so lonely, Rhiannon."

Rhiannon remembered her goal to help this ghost, and did her best to urge Suzanne to move on. "Don't stay here, then. If you call to a loved one, they can meet you on the other side and help you cross over."

The breeze picked up speed and flew around the corner of the partition. Rhiannon followed it and watched as box after box was knocked to the ground.

"What are you doing?" Rhiannon cried out, alarmed at the show of power.

Suzanne made the now empty shelves rattle and shake. Then, just as suddenly as it had started, the wind stopped. "I am tired, Rhiannon. Be my eyes, be my hands."

The voice faded and the air in the room returned to normal. Rhiannon looked at the mess on the floor of the cramped space.

It was wide enough for a twin bed, no, she amended, a cot. Like an army cot. Thin. A cubicle night stand, maybe. And a candle.

A candle?

The place was empty, and if she spread her arms out wide she could almost touch the opposite wall with her fingertips. How could anyone have slept here?

She bent down and picked up a few of the boxes. She sorted through them, looking for clues to who Suzanne was, and why she stayed in the house.

Searching fast, Rhee came up with an old Beatles album cover, but the rest of the stuff was junk. Old screws, nails, and pennies. No secrets. What had Suzanne wanted her to find?

What had she meant, *be her eyes and her hands*?

The back of her neck tickled and she finally became aware of the slow, pulsating bad vibes coming from where the boxes had been on the shelves. Rhiannon quickly put up her shields, hoping to block out anything negative. Her mom would be back any second, and Rhee had some quick thinking to do.

Two separate entities haunted the farmhouse. One who was friendly, and one who was not. Her parents, psychically unavailable, were supposedly safe from harm. Once she had this little situation under control, she'd impress her mom and dad with her new skills and they'd all be back in Vegas by Yuletide.

She tossed the last scraps of faded newspaper into a box,

her nerves on high alert as danger crept closer and closer to her psyche, like high tide at the beach. The only thing that kept her from running was knowing a ghost couldn't physically hurt her. She concentrated on keeping her shields in place as she tried to work.

"Rhiannon."

She jumped, her hand over her mouth to block the scream that was waiting to escape. "Mom!"

"I thought I asked you to clean this up?" Starla plugged in a tall lamp and set the tray of lemonade on the ground. "It looks like a storm came through here! What happened to the shelves?"

Rhiannon picked up a chilled glass. Psychic work always made her thirsty. She drained the cup and eyed the disaster around her feet. Then she looked at the shelves. *Suzanne had been shaking them.*

The boxes were a dud. What about *behind* the boxes? That was where the bad feelings came from. Was there a hidden compartment that held the answers?

Her adrenalin shot up, the fight or flight impulse raged through her bloodstream. *Oh yeah, I'm on to something*, she thought.

Her mom gasped. "You want to bomb something? What are you thinking, Rhee?"

"Mom, stay out of my head, would you?" Rhiannon tapped her finger against her bottom lip. Bombing wasn't a bad idea. Dangerous, though, and no way would her parents go for it.

"Talk to me, honey. You aren't making sense."

She was making perfect sense. Rhee could practically feel the imaginary light bulb go on above her head as she asked, "Hey, do we have a sledgehammer?"

Chapter Seven

"Shopping! I can't believe how much I miss the mall."

"Mom, in case you haven't noticed, this isn't a mall." Rhiannon glanced around at the strip of buildings that had to have been built at the turn of the century.

The three of them stood underneath the Roberts Feed and Tackle sign.

"Now, honey, I think it's quaint. Just look at all the people—"

"I have," Rhiannon said, lifting her chin defensively. She had taken great care picking out her black tights, her plaid mini with short black boots, and her white, cropped sweater. She looked at her mom's amber crinkled broom skirt and the large variety of bead necklaces looped around her neck. Rhee tossed a quick peek at her father, who wore black from head to toe, and sighed. "We are all *way* over-dressed."

Heck, Rhiannon thought. Might as well face the fact that the Godfrey family stood out like a hand *full* of sore thumbs.

So much for blending.

"Honey, don't be that way. Negative attracts more negative—think positive."

Rhiannon noticed her mom's smile was a little wobbly.

"Have you seen these people?" Rhiannon pointed to the women walking up and down the sidewalk and in and out of the shops. The majority wore coverall denim shorts with cotton tank tops. "That hasn't been fashionable since—well, never. And I know that Vogue did not predict the brown work boot to be trendier than a summer sandal."

"Rhee," her dad warned, turning his head to hide a smile.

"What?" She crossed her arms and finished her gawking. The men all seemed to be wearing skin-tight wranglers, cowboy boots and hats, and large belt buckles. She thought of Jared. He'd made the outfit look good, probably because he didn't have a beer belly hanging over his belt. "Ugh."

Her mom took a deep breath. "We look just as different to them. So we're even, balanced. Those boots are probably very comfortable, honey. And the denim coveralls with the daisies embroidered around the top are *darling*."

Rhiannon dropped her arms to her sides and adjusted her purse strap. "I am *so* not buying those jeans. They scream Hicksville!"

"Rhiannon, that's enough. You will be polite."

"Sorry, Daddy." She was being a brat, she knew it, but she didn't fit in here and she didn't want to.

"Remember the Rede. What goes out from you comes back three-fold."

She nodded. She'd been able to recite the Wiccan Rede from the time she was ten, not that she actually believed it, not one-hundred percent. There was some cool stuff in it, but still. Her father's stern look reminded her of what had happened with Maddie.

Had the move been her karmic three-fold punishment? She'd lost her friends, her home, and the institute.

She plastered a smile on her face. "And harm none."

"Wonderful! Well." Starla beamed and shook her hands out to dispel the negative. Her bracelets clinked as she said, "Let's shop."

They entered the Roberts' Feed and Tackle place first. "Do you think that Jared's parents own this store?"

"I don't know. You'll have to ask him the next time you see him."

Rhiannon grimaced. She wasn't wishing for that to happen any time soon. All the weird things going on in her life had made it super clear that a boyfriend was *so* not a good idea. Probably ever.

The store smelled like iron and oil and proudly showcased riding lawn mowers, shovels, hoes and horseshoes. There were large tin tubs that Starla oohed and aahed over, while her dad kept walking around a John Deere mower. All he had to do was kick a tire.

He did.

"Look, Mom. Dad found one he likes."

Her mom giggled without taking her eyes off of the tubs. "Well, there is a lot of grass..."

Rhiannon tapped her foot against the concrete floor. "Mom."

"Hmm?"

"You're drooling."

"What? Oh, that's not funny, Rhiannon. Can't you see these tubs filled with herbs? Basil, oregano, sage..." She laughed with sheer delight. "I can grow my own fennel!"

"That's great, Mom. I'm gonna go next door. Maybe they'll have clothes or something."

"Okay. Do you have money? Buy some things for school."

"I wanna be home schooled, Mom."

Some of the joy left her mom's eyes. "Not happening, sweetie. Good luck finding something."

She'd need it, and they both knew it.

Rhiannon stalked out of the store, wishing she didn't get so mad at her parents. It wasn't enough that she was smart. No, her parents thought she needed to be popular too.

Humph. Like that was gonna happen. She walked by the next shop, which was a bookstore. She could use some more books, she thought as she passed it by. *I'll stop on the way back*, she promised herself.

Rhee kept going until she reached the Brown Bag clothing store. She pushed open the door and the blast of air conditioning nearly took her breath away. She blinked her eyes to adjust them to the fluorescent lights. By the time she could see again, she realized that there was no way that she was going to buy *anything* in here.

Rodeo outfits that looked more like Halloween costumes adorned the walls. Pink ruffled shirts with pearl buttons, raspberry flannel shirts, white beaded belts with mother-of-pearl buckles... She'd landed in fashion hell.

She heard giggling to her left and turned. Three girls, all blonde and tanned, stood together. One of them was holding up a pair of jeans with rhinestones down the sides, while the other two were pointedly staring.

At her.

Again, Rhiannon glanced down at her clothes. Then she jerked her chin up in the air and straightened her spine. She couldn't leave now.

If she did, then those stuck up girls would think they'd chased her from the store. She walked farther in, keeping her stride loose and casual while pretending interest in some hideous bandanas hanging from an antler.

They followed her. The tallest one, who was still shorter than she was, said, "I don't think this is your kind of shop."

Rhiannon pretended not to hear her and hoped that they'd go away.

She leaned over the glass counter and checked out some turquoise jewelry. She hated confrontations, hated them, hated them.

"Can I help you, hon?" The lady behind the counter gave her a sympathetic smile.

"Uh." Rhee started shaking. She just wanted to go home. But she couldn't let anybody see that she was scared. She was Rhiannon Selene Godfrey, and she wouldn't be intimidated by a bunch of bullies in designer buckskin.

She quickly glanced at the stuff beneath the glass counter. "I'd like to see those earrings, please."

"These?" The woman pulled out a pair of chandelier style earrings, sage green turquoise set in spun silver.

"Yeah. Those are really pretty." And they were. Tanya would think so too. "I'll take two pair."

"They'll look great on you. But I have something I think you'd really like. It would go perfect with what you have on now. I swear you look like you've stepped out of a magazine."

The girls snickered and Rhiannon felt the color creeping up her cheeks. "Oh, well, okay. Thanks. I think."

The lady laughed and brought out some silver charm bracelets. "These have been really popular with the other kids around here. They buy the first letter of the name of their boyfriends."

Rhiannon tried not to hear the mean giggling from behind

the cowboy shirts.

The saleslady raised her voice. "Some girls have a lot more charms than others, now, but I don't suppose that will be a problem with you."

"Hmm?" Bless the Goddess, she just wanted to make a beeline for the door.

"Well, you're really pretty, hon. All that long red wavy hair, it makes you unique too. Lots of guys like that, especially when everybody else looks just the same."

The woman jerked her head to where the giggles had stopped like someone had pushed a button.

"Thank you." Rhiannon bit the inside of her cheek before she laughed out loud. She paid for her items, then kept her eyes trained on the door.

She'd shopped, she'd paid, she could leave.

Rhee was halfway through the store when a leather-studded belt fell at her feet.

"Oops! Dropped that, could you get it for me?"

Rhiannon inhaled through her nose to keep her cool. She'd be willing to bet a silver dollar that Miss Mouth and her friends were the same age as she was. And to think these were the people her mom wanted her to make friends with.

Should she pick the belt up and get out?

Or should she keep on walking? Using her telepathy wasn't really an option.

"Helllooo," the girl practically sang. "I was talking to you. Are you deaf?"

The Rede. Remember the Rede. Rhiannon stepped over the belt and walked toward the door and peace.

The girl made the mistake of grabbing her by the arm. Rhiannon turned on one pointed high heel, expelling a rush of air. She'd be polite, but she wouldn't be pushed. "Let go of me."

The girl dropped her hand, then smirked. "I just asked you a question."

Rhiannon wanted to melt beneath the cruel gazes of the three blondes, but knew instinctively that she had to act tough. "Funny. I didn't hear anything."

"What?" The surprised look on the girl's face was sort of comical.

Rhee gulped past the tension building from her toes up. She had to get out of the store before she did something that she would probably regret. "No, I won't pick up the belt you dropped in front of me. Excuse me." Rhiannon brushed past, two steps closer to freedom.

They converged like a pack of wolves in front of her. The leader of the pack growled, "Where are you from? Are you on vacation?"

Rhee lifted her brow as she'd seen her father do a trillion times, "Vacation? Here? I don't think so." She twitched her lips and stuck her nose a little higher in the air to let them know what she thought of their little suburb. "We just moved from Vegas."

The girls nodded, as if that explained everything.

Rhiannon could feel her temper bubbling, which was never a good sign. The rack of post cards near the front door turned as if pushed by an invisible finger. She tightened her grip on her bag, pinching the thin skin next to her thumb.

Her parents would never forgive her if she dumped the entire stock of rhinestone clothes down on these girls' heads. What goes around, come around—three-fold. *Remember Maddie Johnson.*

She sighed, then softened her tone. *I don't need any new*

enemies. "Sorry, that was sarcastic. I'm Rhiannon Godfrey. I'll be going to high school here."

The back-up girls giggled and the tallest blonde narrowed her sharp green eyes. "Interesting." She turned to her friends. "I think we ought to give Brianna a real, old-fashioned kind of Crystal Lake welcome."

Rhiannon didn't care for the look on the girl's face and quickly inhaled before she ended up pulling out the chick's hair by the roots. She doubled her efforts to control her irritation.

"My name is Rhiannon, not Brianna. I have to get going. My parents are waiting for me." Why had she said that? It made her sound like a five-year old. It was no wonder she wasn't cool.

"We'll look for you at school—give you a tour, make you feel right at home, won't we?" The blonde grinned and her friends kept nodding like brainless bobble-heads.

Then the girl pivoted on her cowboy boot heel, sending a cloud of perfume toward Rhiannon as all three of them pushed by her to get out the door.

Rhee refused to move an eyelash until they were gone. Even then, she waited a few minutes until she felt calm enough to stay in control. Looking down, she saw that she'd been gripping her bag so tight she'd made bloody half-moons in her palms with her fingernails.

Then her shoulders slumped and she felt like a deflated helium balloon. *If this was normal high school behavior, she wouldn't survive freshman year.* Rhee pushed on the door, stumbled over the metal strip on the ground and bumped into her parents on the sidewalk.

"Oof! Sorry, I—"

"Rhee! How'd you do?"

She got her balance, yanked her bangs out of her face and

lifted the bag. "I found jewelry, can't go wrong there. Mom, I don't want to go to—"

Starla said, "Honey, look who we met up with again..."

Rhiannon wished she could disappear. How'd she miss her mom's hostess voice? She looked up, squinting against the sun, and sure enough, there was Jared.

"Hey, Rhiannon. What's up?"

Had he seen her stumble out of the store? *Great.* "Jared. I'm good. Shopping." Tongue-tied again. She could blame her blush on the sun.

Starla said, "He's here with his sister and some of her friends. Have you seen a pretty blonde?"

Rhiannon had to bite the inside of her cheek to avoid asking if the blonde had the forked tongue of a poisonous rattlesnake. She should have recognized the grass green eyes. How could Jared, who was cool and awesome as well as cute, have a sister who was such a...a...a Barbie?

Her mom was saying, "We just got here. Rhee?"

"Uh. There were some girls inside the shop. You must have missed them."

No such luck. The girl's voice carried down the sidewalk like an evil wind. Rhiannon made sure to keep her back to her.

"Jared! I've been looking all over for you—you were supposed to be waiting by the truck. Mom said Dad was ready to leave a half hour ago. Where were you?"

"Bookstore."

And to think, Rhiannon gave herself a swift mental kick, *that I just walked right by that place in order to look at clothes.* She really needed to examine her instincts a little closer.

Rhiannon turned around to face Jared's sister, who came to a screeching halt on the cement next to where they all were standing.

Rhee smiled sweetly and held up her shopping bag, even though she felt like puking. She hated confrontations. Hated feeling awkward.

"Uh." The girl stared at Starla's brightly layered beads then glanced at Miles and his dark clothes before she finally settled her gaze back on Jared.

It was amazing, Rhee thought. The girl obviously had a brain hidden behind the streaked blonde hair. She brightened her smile and oozed charm like a squished Twinkie.

Rhiannon was reluctantly impressed as she gushed, "You must be the Godfreys! Jared said he met you last week, when he returned your cow. He didn't mention...well, he just said that you all were very nice."

Starla smiled with good will. "And you are?"

The girl stuck out her hand and shot a glance at Rhiannon. "I'm Janet, Mrs. Godfrey, and I am so *pleased* to meet you."

Rhiannon stepped forward, her fingers itching. She would not put up with anyone mocking her mother!

Jared got there before her.

"C'mon, Janet. Oh, wait. Did you all get a chance to meet Rhiannon? She'll be going to Crystal Lake High too."

Janet smiled, showing off a dimple in her left cheek. "Yeah, we met already. Inside the store."

Rhiannon flattened her lips, recognizing the false friendliness Jared's twin exuded. "That's right. I think you mentioned a welcoming party?"

Janet's friends, still un-introduced, gave fake waves with just the tip of their fingers.

Jared looked from Rhiannon to his sister, sensing something wrong, no doubt. Well, she wasn't going to explain.

"Time to go," Rhiannon said, turning her back on the others to face her parents. They stared at her as if she'd grown an extra nose.

"That was rude, Rhiannon," her mother whispered.

She waited until she could tell they were gone before saying angrily, "I hate this place. I will never belong here, and I am *so* not going to school with that prima donna."

"But, honey..." Her mother was at a loss for words.

Rhiannon grabbed her dad's forearm and pleaded, "Please? Can you at least think about it some more before you register me? I know that you feel I need social interaction. I'll, like, volunteer at the nursing home or whatever, work at the hospital, anything but have to face that horrible, nasty bi—"

Her mom's crystal necklace glowed off and on as if it had a faulty wire, and her dad's bolo tie bobbed up and down against his chest.

"Stop it!" Miles sighed as he slapped his hand over the tie. "Calm down, Rhee. We'll talk about it when we get home. We are already a spectacle without having a family argument in the middle of the parking lot."

Her heart leapt toward the reprieve. "Thank you, Dad."

Her mom muttered, "I need my herbal tea. My crystals. My divination candle. We can't have made a mistake about this, Miles. We were so sure."

They were all quiet as they drove home. Rhiannon didn't care about the ghost, she didn't care about the farmhouse or Betsy the cow. There was only one place where she really and truly was safe from the world. The institute.

Chapter Eight

High School. Just saying the words out loud made her stomach clench and her head ache. She only had two days left until her real torture began.

She must have been doing some really bad things for all this rotten crappy stuff to be happening to her. Hadn't she been punished enough already?

Her mother had dealt the tarot cards, her father had done a numerology reading, and that was that. She had to go to school.

Rhee had no choice but to give her parents the cold shoulder, on principle. And with Tanya still in England, she had to relent and talk to Matthew over email. Which had been a stupid idea, since all he wanted to do was tell Mrs. Edwards and Dr. Richards about the farmhouse being haunted.

Nobody understood where she was coming from.

She got off the edge of her bed, her bare feet sinking into the plush white area rug they'd placed on the wood floor.

Her parents hadn't liked the idea of tearing down the partition in the attic, so they'd painted and cleaned instead. Rhee was now the proud owner of a closet she was afraid to go into, but at least it had a door and a lock. She wished they'd let her take a sledgehammer to it.

"Where are you, Suzanne?"

Rhiannon sat down in the recliner chair next to the window. The spirit hadn't been heard from since the shelf incident.

Too unsettled to read a book, Rhee got up and paced the room.

"I suppose I could go and search the storage barn for clues on who used to live here. Dad's been cleaning it out, and Mom said he found some cool stuff."

The gauze curtains at her window fluttered. Rhiannon glanced around hopefully. "Suzanne?"

Nothing. She stared at the drapes, but they didn't budge. It must have been her imagination.

"Girl, you have got to get out of this house. You are talking to yourself *and* seeing things."

She grabbed her black Doc Martens and quickly laced them up. She ran down the stairs two at a time, listening for her mom and dad. She didn't want to tell them where she was going—in fact, she didn't want to talk to them at all.

Ever.

The barn was open when she passed by, and she poked her head in the door. *All clear.*

"Hey, Betsy." She scratched behind the cow's ears. "I wish you could go with me to check out the outbuildings. I'm looking for treasure."

Rhiannon felt a little silly talking about treasure, but what the heck. She was bored.

"So, are you ready to move into a new place? Dad's getting the best of the barn thingies all ready for you. You can live like a queen."

Betsy's tail swished and her eyes closed.

"Are you lonely? Do we need to get you a king cow?"

Betsy cracked open one eye and chewed her cud while blowing hot air through her nostrils.

Rhiannon laughed. "I'll take that as a no. Well, you'll be happy, Betsy, that's the important thing. And Mom will be happy, opening her store in here once everything has been fumigated. And Dad is already happy, pretending to be Farmer John. Which just leaves me. Unhappy. Why did we have to move?"

The sound of her dad's riding mower close to the barn cut off her pity party.

She waved good-bye to the cow and ran to the outbuilding that was being used as a place to pile all the unwanted stuff.

Rhee paused outside the unpainted structure and eyed the padlock. Did she really want to paw through someone else's junk?

"Yes," she answered herself. She focused on the shiny new lock until she heard the click. Imagining the lock open made it happen for real.

She pushed open the squeaking door, then used her telepathy to switch on the light. Rhee had to work with what was available—in this case, it was a forty-watt bulb when a hundred watt was needed.

"Dang." Craning her head back, she saw boxes as high as the ceiling tilting precariously to the side, defying gravity. Dust motes danced like bugs in front of her eyes, the smell was musty and...just plain old.

She could see where her dad had added to the previous stacks, right up close next to the door. The Godfreys needed to have a garage sale. Garage included.

Rhiannon made her way, carefully, through the trail that led to the back. The light didn't shine very far and the shadows flickered and moved, which gave her the creeps.

"Where to start?" Rhee didn't care for the way her voice echoed around her. In hind sight, it hadn't been such a great idea staying up all night and watching Stephen King movies.

"Shake it off, Rhiannon. Movies are pretend. Ghosts aren't scary." *Liar, liar, pants on fire.* She forced herself to think about Suzanne. Where could she find the spirit's secrets?

"The oldest stuff will be in the way back, of course. I mean, how old is the farmhouse? A hundred years? That's a lot of junk."

She heard a sound to her left and whirled. A box at the top of a stack teetered, then tottered, and Rhiannon held her breath. With a flick of her mind, she pictured the box safely balanced and exhaled. She should have been filled with relief, but she knew she wasn't alone. *Stop psyching yourself out! One too many horror movies, Rhee.* Mind-numbing fear was just a heartbeat away. "Suzanne?"

There is nothing to be afraid of. Rhee carefully walked between the boxes, her steps slow. If she gave in to fear, she'd never find the answers she needed. She peeked around the box, looking for whatever made the noise. A falling leaf? The sound of the boxes settling? *Nope.* Two yellow eyes peered at her from a dark crevice. The eyes grew wider and she couldn't stop a scream as the thing darted toward her.

"Ah!"

She tripped over her own feet and landed hard on her backside as a rat the size of a full grown cat scampered by her. It was close enough that she could see its whiskers twitch and its tail slide like a worm across the packed dirt floor.

Rhiannon exhaled, her temper rising as the scare wore off, leaving her to feel a little ridiculous. "Come back here, you dirty rodent!"

Didn't rats carry the plague or something?

Using all of her concentration she focused on the brownish gray fur of the quivering rat. Slowly, it slid her way and she turned it, raising it about a foot off the ground so they'd be eye to eye.

"Listen, pal. You got me. I coulda had a heart attack, and I'm only fourteen."

The rat's nose wiggled and its little eyes darted back and forth as it tried to get out of her psychic hold.

Rhiannon's anger ebbed. "Okay, so maybe I scared you too. We can make a deal, all right? You stay out of my way, and I'll stay out of yours."

The rat's body became very still, as if it understood her perfectly. "Wouldn't that be a riot? Being able to talk to animals? Well, I have enough problems, bud. You have no idea."

She released her grip on the rodent, who, once free, took a minute to sit back on its haunches and stare at her with its beady, black eyes.

"Scoot!" Rhiannon said.

The rat took off.

"Well." She stood, brushed her butt off with both hands and headed toward the door and the farmhouse.

It was obvious she just wasn't cut out to be Indiana Jones.

Rhee was so focused on getting the heck out that it took a second before she noticed the stack of junk in front of her was swaying. One box fell to the left, and the other was falling to the right. In what seemed like slow motion, Rhiannon could only watch as the box came straight for her head—she was as powerless to move as the rat had been in her psychic grip.

I'll be crushed to oblivion!

Rhee felt two hands in the small of her back push her out of the way and she skidded forward, landing on her hands and knees. She turned just in time to see the box crash and burst open like a ripe watermelon.

What the heck had that been? Who had saved her? Why hadn't she been able to stop the box from falling? Her psychic powers had been frozen, a thing that had never happened to her before. The closest thing she could think of to describe the feeling was that ickiness from her closet.

Rhiannon swallowed, her throat dry. She sat there, trying to regain a little dignity. "For who, Rhee? The dang rat?"

She got to her feet, again, and rubbed her hands together. Her palms were bleeding, and her jeans now had a cool hole in the left knee. Well, cool if her mom could get the bloodstain out.

What if my powers are gone for good? She deliberately concentrated on a broken shovel propped against the wall. She focused, narrowing her eyes and imagining a string between her and the shovel, bringing the tool to her. It worked, no prob.

"Weird," she said as she held onto the shovel. Why had her powers deserted her, especially when she needed them to stop the box from landing on her head?

The box. Equally curious and afraid, she walked to the split-open container. "What's in here? Something important?" Talking out loud made her feel less alone, although it was a terrible habit. But a common one with only children. Dr. Richards said so.

She listened, but nobody answered with either a deed or a word. "Hey, what's that?" She dropped down to one knee, her right one, and saw a plain brown paper package. In the fall the brown paper had peeled back, revealing a statue, which should have broken, but hadn't. She reached her hands in and pulled it out. "A jewelry box." She carefully put it next to her on the ground, as if it were made of solid gold.

It wasn't. It was pink porcelain and girly with a ballerina on the lid. She continued pawing through the box in search of more loot. A thin, faded Sears and Roebucks catalogue from, whoa, 1900. "Suzanne's?"

She pulled away more brown paper and rescued a hatbox. *This is just like Grandma Godfrey's,* she thought. *I could use it for hair ties, once I clean it up.* She noticed the dirt caked on her hands and hesitated to plunge them back inside the box.

Well, after all these years, what was a little more dirt?

She pushed aside old linen hand towels with monograms that were moth eaten and disgusting. Maybe there nothing left to find. Glancing at her three treasures, she was so happy she thought she might burst. If treasure hunting offered a medical plan and a 401K, she could consider switching careers.

Really thirsty now, she carefully wrapped up her treasures in the old brown paper and nudged the practically empty box to one side.

"Not a bad haul for the first time treasure hunting." *If it wasn't for almost being squished...*

The sound of another box shaking at the top of a different stack had her grabbing her stuff and running for the door. "Okay, okay—I'm outta here!"

Rhee made her way back to the house as if she were a spy on a secret mission, but she was busted the second she came in through the laundry room.

Her mom called from the kitchen, "Rhiannon, UPS arrived, and your new clothes are here!"

She stopped in her tracks, frantically looking around for a place to hide her treasures. *Under the cabinet,* she thought as she opened the door and shoved her stuff in behind all the cleaning supplies.

"Be right there, Mom." *And then I'll come back for you, my pretties.*

"I'm here, you don't have to shout."

Rhiannon scrambled to her feet and raised her eyes. Her mom was smiling and holding a giant box.

"Truce?" Starla asked with a knowing grin.

Sighing, Rhiannon thought of all the fabulous clothes she'd bought over the internet that were tucked inside.

Abercrombie, Gap, Old Navy, Pac Sun, Hot Topic and more.

She bit her lip, knowing her pride was going to have to take a hike.

"Sure. Truce. I'll be the best dressed freak in Hicksville."

At her mom's disapproving look, she amended, "Um, I meant, Crystal Lake High School."

Chapter Nine

She woke up feeling like she'd had too much junk food. Sick to her stomach, tired, and scared. Her people skills sucked and she'd never been to a real classroom in her life.

The kids were going to kill her, like in that *Lord of the Flies* movie.

She could see it now. Her temper would be out of control, and she just might send another teacher screaming into the hallway, in need of therapy and Prozac. Maybe even a straight jacket.

She wished she could blame her parents, but she knew they were only doing what they felt was right for her.

Would they be sorry, or what, when she came home dead?

She slapped at the alarm clock next to her bed, then mentally flipped on the lights. The room was bright as day and, man, she wanted nothing more than to hide her head under the covers.

"Rhee?" Her mom opened the door, carrying a tray that held a pot of tea and a new kind of muffin she was experimenting with.

Rhiannon's stomach lurched. So far Betsy was the only one liking them. Bran and soy with carrot chunks. *Yuck.*

"Morning, honey. Rise and shine, and may the blessing of the Goddess be with you today."

"I'm gonna need all the help I can get, Mom."

Her mom opted to ignore her complaint. "Do you know what you're going to wear?"

Irritated at her mom's excited-to-be-alive attitude, Rhiannon let her own temper flare. "Geez! If you're so excited about school, why don't you go?"

She was sorry the second she said it, and wished she could keep the mean things that sometimes slipped from her mouth buried behind her tongue where they belonged. Her mom looked hurt, and Rhee knew it was her fault.

So sue me, she thought.

"Zoomies?" Starla, obviously willing to forgive and forget, smiled brightly. "The shirt you got from there was darling. Good choice. I know you don't want to go to school. But, honey, I think it is going to be a wonderful experience. You'll have to be on guard for a while, but it will get easier, you know, the more you practice."

Her mom put the tray on the table next to the computer. "I made you something for today."

Seeing the hopeful smile on her mom's face, Rhee knew that whatever it was, no matter how ugly or horrid, she had better be nice.

"Here."

"Oh!" Rhiannon felt the power of the amulet as her mom placed the necklace in her palm. Her fingers closed over the milky white pendant in the shape of a crescent moon. "This is great; I love it, Mom!" And she did too.

"I've been saving it. It was blessed by the coven before we moved here. In fact, Tisha sends her love. I spoke to her already this morning."

Mom must be super stressed if she's already talking to the High Priestess this early, Rhiannon thought as she slipped the thin silver chain over her head.

"Tell her I said hi back." Rhiannon looked in the mirror. The pendant practically glowed. She gave her mom a hug. "Thanks."

Her mom clapped her hands, she was so happy. Of course, her mom was just that way. Happy, all the frickin' time. "Come on down when you're dressed. Your dad's ready to drive you to school."

Rhiannon held her smile in place but groaned once her mom left. It had been a toss up to see which was worse—taking the yellow school bus, or having her parents drive her in their new burgundy minivan that said "Celestial Beginnings" on the side, complete with glittering gold stars and wands.

She'd chosen to ride with her parents, knowing that at least they wouldn't throw stuff at her or call her a freak.

It took practically forever, but she finally decided on black jeans from Abercrombie, a plain black fitted T-shirt from the Gap, and black Converse sneakers. The fashion experts all said you could never go wrong with black.

The silver chain and the moonstone pendant twinkled.

She left her long red hair loose, letting it fall in waves to her waist. Rhee carefully applied dark brown eyeliner beneath her blue eyes, and swiped a little mascara on too.

Turning at every conceivable angle to get a good look at herself in her mirror, she couldn't find a single fixable flaw. Tall and skinny, she couldn't wave a magic wand and give herself curves. Her teeth, while white, were too big. Her stomach tightened with nerves. She didn't look like a psychic freak, but people had a way of knowing when someone else was different.

Like they could sense it.

She spritzed jade water mixed with chamomile and lavender on her hair and clothes. Jade was for solidity of identity—her mom said it was especially good for teenagers—and the chamomile and lavender were for calm.

Her palms were all sweaty and she hadn't even gone downstairs yet, so she really hoped the potion would kick in fast.

Panic rose as she thought of school. Would the hallways be crowded with kids pushing and shoving? Would she be taped to a pole or dumped in a trashcan?

Oh man, oh man...would she get lost? She'd studied the layout of the school and knew where her classes were by heart. Her mom had sprinkled rosemary on it for remembrance.

Rhiannon was as prepared as she could be.

But she was still terrified.

By the time they pulled up in front of the brick school building, Rhiannon wasn't sure who was more nervous. Her mom, who was bubbling with tension, or her dad, who held onto the steering wheel as if it were a lifeline, or herself.

Miss Gurgling Guts.

She wanted to curl into a little ball and hide beneath the seat. She could hitchhike back to Vegas and hope that her parents would just forget they ever had a daughter.

Right.

She gripped her backpack, opened the side door and slid out. Pretending to be calm, uh-huh. "See ya."

Her mom's face was pinched with last minute doubts. "Call us, honey, if you need to. Send us a thought. Let us know that you're okay."

"I thought that I was supposed to be normal. No telepathy,

no opening things with my mind and no frightening the other students with flying objects."

Her mom's chin trembled. "You know what I mean."

Her dad said, "Hail and farewell, Rhiannon," then blew her a kiss, which she didn't return, and she shut the door.

Okay. She *slammed* the door and watched her parents drive away.

Then turned and promptly smacked into another body, sending books and pencils everywhere.

So much for controlling the objects around me, Rhee thought nervously. That had to be some kind of record for losing control—not even a full second!

"I'm sorry," Rhiannon said to the back of the girl's light brown hair. She was crouched down on all fours, scrambling to pick up scattered books and pens.

"My fault," the girl mumbled without looking up, "my fault. I never look where I'm going, and I hope I didn't break anything of yours, and..."

"Hang on," Rhiannon broke in, relieved. The exploding pens and paper had been an accident? *Not my fault.*

"No, really, I always run into people."

The girl quickly raised her face, and Rhiannon noticed that she had plump chipmunk cheeks and round glasses that had slid to the end of her cute pug nose.

Two braids, one on either side of her face, fell to chin level. She had on a large flannel shirt and jeans, even though the weather was still warm. Rhee could tell right away that this girl wasn't one of the popular kids.

Which, so far as Rhee was concerned, made her a good candidate for the "find a friend" game.

The girl stood up, but Rhee still towered over her by about

five inches. Feeling like a giant, Rhee handed the girl the book she'd picked up from the sidewalk. "Here."

"Thanks," the girl mumbled.

Taking a deep breath, Rhiannon imagined she was speaking in front of a large auditorium of psychic researchers. That would be easier than talking to a stranger who had the power to ridicule her. "Hi, I'm Rhiannon."

She saw the flash of surprise on the girl's face as she bundled her backpack to her chest, and inadvertently picked up, "*You're talking to me?*"

So understanding that sentiment, Rhiannon smiled. *No psychic flashes!*

"I'm Bonnie."

"Do you know where room 101 is? I've got math, and I'd hate to be late on the first day."

Bonnie's cheeks got blotchy. "I have math too."

Rhiannon could tell Bonnie was painfully shy. And plain, but nothing that a mini makeover couldn't fix. Rhee stole a peek at Bonnie's flannel shirt. Maybe a shopping spree too.

Rhiannon adjusted her backpack. "So, can I walk with you?"

Bonnie dropped her eyes and shrugged. "Sure."

When they reached the math class, it was already three quarters of the way full. Rhiannon was so nervous that it took every bit of courage she had to enter the room. It seemed like all the kids were staring at her.

Maybe because they were.

Well, she wasn't going to walk around with her eyes on the ground, like Bonnie was doing. No wonder the girl ran into everybody!

She tossed her hair back with pumped-up confidence.

Whether people liked it or not, her hair was auburn red, long, and definitely caught the eye. It was different, just like her. She casually strode inside, in front of the gawking kids in the first row, and down the path between the other desks.

Bonnie had picked a seat in the back, and Rhiannon dropped her backpack down on the one next to it.

Bonnie gave her a shy smile.

Which Rhiannon returned, and, still smiling, glanced toward the door. There was Jared.

Wow. He wasn't wearing a cowboy hat and his hair was sun-bleached blond. He wore jeans, sneakers, and some country band T-shirt. Definitely a ten out of ten on the cute scale.

It seemed like everyone in the class knew Jared, liked Jared, and wanted to sit by Jared.

Too cool for me, Rhiannon thought as she looked away before he caught her staring at him.

Of course, his friends had saved him a seat in the center of the class, and he never even noticed she was in the same room.

And even if he had noticed, Rhiannon Godfrey, what makes you think he would have said hi?

She forced those thoughts away as the teacher walked in, and tried to concentrate on her first real math class.

Miss Walsh clapped her hands for silence as soon as the bell rang.

"Good morning! Welcome, freshmen, to high school. Since this is your first class of the day, this will be your homeroom."

Rhiannon stole a look at Jared, who was fiddling with a pencil.

"I expect for this to be a terrific year. Let's begin by introducing ourselves!"

Rhiannon froze. *Sheesh.* What a way to make sure that everybody's eyes would be on her. Great. She hoped she didn't make anything fly around the room. *Concentrate, Rhee, focus.*

She was in the last row, the last chair. Maybe everybody would be bored by then and not look at her.

It was obvious that most of these kids had all known each other from practically preschool and they had a bond.

She was the one who didn't belong.

Of course, when Jared stood up and introduced himself, he was totally cool.

Then it was Bonnie's turn and Rhiannon felt sorta sorry for her. Bonnie kept her eyes on the desk top and tripped over the chair leg as she stood and mumbled, "Hi, I'm Bonnie."

Miss Walsh asked her to speak clearly, which only made Bonnie more uncomfortable.

Then her new maybe-friend plopped into her seat and sent her book bag crashing to the ground, and a bunch of the kids laughed. *Jerks.*

Rhiannon wished she could send Bonnie courage, but she'd promised to keep her abilities to herself. Maybe a small telepathic vote of confidence?

And then the teacher announced, "I see here we have someone from out of state! Rhiannon Godfrey, please stand up...it says that you've been home-schooled." The teacher arched her brow. "Class, make sure and help Rhiannon here out with schedules, finding her classes, etcetera."

Miss Walsh smiled and Rhiannon wanted to crawl beneath the desk. Her insides were all nervous and jiggly, and then the paper tray flipped over on Miss Walsh's desk and Rhiannon panicked. *Did I do that? Oh man, control, control!*

The teacher sighed, "This is the third time today I've

knocked that darn thing over."

Rhiannon relaxed in her seat. *Not my fault,* she thought as Miss Walsh said, "It will be interesting to see how you do here."

Rhiannon swallowed the urge to explain that she wasn't a science experiment. She'd left all experimentation back at the institute.

She got to her feet and felt the force of everyone's gaze. Pinching the skin between her thumb and finger, she unstuck her tongue from the roof of her mouth and tried to speak clearly, "Uh, I'm Rhiannon; we just moved from Vegas."

"Explains the gothic look," somebody said with a snicker.

Rhee jerked her chin in the air and tightened her lips. Focus, focus. "It's nice to be here."

By the Goddess, how lame was that, she thought as she sat back down, her eyes straight ahead.

Jared turned and said, "Hey, Rhiannon! I didn't see you back there. Welcome to Crystal Lake High, home of the Warriors."

Her cheeks had to look like twin tomatoes she was so embarrassed. She managed to squeak out, "Hey."

An awkward silence settled over the class as everybody watched the exchange between cool kid and new freak kid.

Rhee wanted to drop her head to her desk and die.

Chapter Ten

Lunch. She'd love to meet the psychotic jerk who'd thought up the unique torture of the lunchroom.

Rhiannon's palms were sweaty as she looked at the long line of kids waiting to get a tray, get food, and then find a seat at a table with their friends.

Problems came from every direction. Her hands were too slick to hold a tray without dropping it, she was a vegetarian and didn't eat Meat Loaf Surprise, and the biggest obstacle— *drum roll, please*—she didn't have any friends.

She swallowed and joined the end of the line. When a person was scared, Dr. Richards always said the best thing to do was step back and prioritize. She should have realized that a country school would not have a gourmet cafeteria. She could eat an apple for lunch, and drink a carton of milk. Neither of those items required a tray. Her shoulders relaxed a fraction on an inch.

If she walked slowly, maybe the bell would ring and she wouldn't be stuck looking for a table. Maybe nobody would notice if she just kept walking around the cafeteria with her apple and her milk. Maybe she could find Bonnie, and Bonnie wouldn't mind if she sat down at her table.

This was the worst kind of humiliation. Kids had steered clear of her; she hadn't had any more classes with Bonnie or

Jared, and she'd sat alone in the back like she didn't care. Man, it sucked to know that she did care. A lot.

She stepped forward in the line.

"Look, everybody!"

Rhiannon's pulse jumped, her senses warned her to beware. She turned quickly and saw Janet, her two friends from the Brown Bag and a few others. Janet had a big, plastic smile on her face, which Rhee knew was trouble.

"Hey!" Janet said loudly. "It's that gothic witch from Las Vegas I was telling you about."

Rhiannon could feel her cheeks burn as everybody laughed. *It seems like there are worse humiliations than not having friends.*

Having enemies went right to the top of the list.

She stuffed her hands in her pockets before she caused harm ("Harm ye none", she whispered under her breath) and stood, rooted to the linoleum floor of the cafeteria.

Run. Just run.

She'd never live this down. She was never coming back. What difference did it make if she threw up in front of everybody?

Janet moved closer. "Remember that special Crystal Lake welcome I promised you? Well, here it is!" Janet took an open milk carton and dumped it all over Rhiannon's brand-new Converse.

Silence. Then an explosion of laughter.

She felt the power surge from her fingertips and curled them deeper in her pockets. Anger, embarrassment, and the fact that she was on the verge of losing it big time made her calm on the outside, even though she was a crackling mess on the inside.

She met Janet's green eyes and spoke softly. "You'll regret that."

Janet's mean smile fell from her face, but Rhiannon didn't care. She speed-walked out of the lunchroom, the sound of squishy milk in her sneakers an echo of the cruelty close on her heels.

Rhee barely made it to the bathroom before losing control; her vision was blurry with unshed tears. She opened the door, minus her hands, and stalked over to the row of sinks, hoping that nobody was in the stalls.

All around her things went crazy. The paper towel dispenser unraveled, the stall doors banged open and shut. *Control yourself, Rhiannon!* But it was so hard, when she really wanted to have a good, old-fashioned temper tantrum. Which, considering her powers, could be a bad thing.

The toilet lids slammed open and shut, but the noise wasn't making her feel any better.

She turned on the water in the sink full blast and stuck her wrists beneath the cold stream. Rhee sniffed, then caught a sob in her throat when she saw her image in the mirror. *I'm just a girl.*

Why does Janet hate me so much?

The door to the bathroom opened again, but this time she had nothing to do with it. Her mind froze and everything stopped banging at once.

She quickly hid her face behind her hair, determined to keep her tears to herself. Maybe whoever just walked in wouldn't notice the mess. Right.

"Hey, are you okay?"

She recognized Bonnie's voice, timid and kind.

"Yeah. Fine," Rhiannon whispered without raising her eyes.

Just want to die of embarrassment, thanks. She couldn't look at Bonnie, she was just too humiliated.

"Bunch of nasty cats. Don't let them bother you."

This voice was new, firm, and confident.

Rhiannon lifted her head and met the almond-shaped brown eyes of a beautiful Native American girl. Her hair was longer than Rhiannon's, and cut in a straight edge at her waist. No bangs, either.

Bonnie came forward, tiptoeing around the mounds of paper towels on the floor. She tore a sheet off and handed it to Rhiannon. "Here."

"Thanks."

"Sure." Bonnie glanced around the bathroom. "I was looking for you in the lunchroom, wondering if you wanted to sit with us."

Bonnie's expression told her that she had expected for the answer to be no. But now...now she'd seen that her offer would be doing Rhiannon a favor.

Rhee sniffed one last time and fixed the smudge of eyeliner beneath her lid. *As if people were lining up to sit with me,* she thought.

The other girl crossed her arms over her chest and lifted her lips in a partial grin. "I'm Melody. You might want to wipe the milk off your shoes, or they'll start to stink."

Rhiannon glanced down at the tops of her sneakers and wiggled her wet toes. "Good idea."

"You know," Melody continued, "Janet and her minions will eventually forget about you. Until then, you should probably just stay out of her way."

She dabbed a wet paper towel on her laces and told a bald-faced lie. "Janet doesn't scare me."

Melody grinned fully, showing a broad smile and braces. "That's not the point. The point is that for whatever reason—I'm thinking insane, ravaging jealousy—Janet has decided that she hates you. Sooo, she'll make your life a living hell just because she can."

"What makes her so special?" Rhee stiffened.

Bonnie laughed, and Melody dropped her arms to her sides. "Duh. Her last name is *Roberts*. Her family founded Crystal Lake, and she never lets anyone forget it."

"But Jared isn't like that."

Bonnie sighed. "How do you know Jared?"

"He returned our cow—long story."

Rhiannon threw the wadded up paper towels into the trash and added, "He seems really nice. But Janet and her friends, well, we met at the Brown Bag, shopping, before school even started. She didn't like me from the minute I walked in the door."

Melody nodded. "You're pretty. You dress cool. And you are from somewhere besides Crystal Lake."

Bonnie agreed, as if these were valid reasons for ruining someone's life. "True. All of it."

Rhiannon squirmed. "This is how everyone I know dresses. I've never seen so many people in coveralls and cowboy boots in my life."

Bonnie tugged self-consciously at her flannel shirt. Melody looked down at her boots and shrugged. "I like my boots, and jeans are comfortable."

She thought of all her magazines and the glossy pages of make-up and styles. "You should wear what you like. I mean—" she pointed to Melody's white shirt, "—you don't look like you're going to the rodeo or anything."

Melody pretended to be shocked and gasped. "Not go to the Crystal Lake rodeo? Girl, you have a lot to learn if you want to fit in around here."

Bonnie said, "The rodeo is in October, and there's a parade down Main Street, hay rides, a carnival, and of course each grade gets to crown a prince and princess, well, except for the seniors. They get to crown a king and queen."

Melody interrupted, "And of course Janet will want to be princess of ninth grade. She was talking about it all last year, even."

Rhiannon groaned. "Princess? Isn't that a little, um, dumb?"

"Not in Crystal Lake. Then we have football season, and homecoming, and..."

"Stop! I was home-schooled, remember? This is too much."

"Why didn't you go to a regular school?" Melody asked.

"Uh..." She and her parents had rehearsed this part, which was sorta true. "Too much traveling. My mom, she was in advertising."

"Oh."

Melody and Bonnie shared a look but didn't ask any more questions. Finally, Bonnie said, "I'm starving, do you want to sit with us?"

Rhiannon nodded. Grateful. Ready to get down on her knees and say thanks. She only smiled. "Um, is the line still going to be open?"

"Oh, you can share with me. My mom always packs enough for a small army. Which is why I'm fat."

Melody smacked her friend. "You are not fat. You have big boobs, which isn't the same."

Rhiannon looked down at her own chest, which was

practically non-existent. Her mom said that would change since she started her monthlies, but so far, no growth. Then she glanced at Bonnie's tent-like shirt and wondered if she wasn't better off.

Melody opened the door, and she and Bonnie trailed behind. Melody was still giving her friend a lecture on the evils of letting your mother run your life.

"C'mon, Bonnie. You're fourteen, and you've never even picked out your own clothes. Your mom packs your lunch, tells you what you can watch on TV, and won't let you have a cell phone."

Rhiannon looked at Bonnie through different eyes. Melody continued, "All you do is play with your dogs."

"I like my dogs!"

"They slobber. Whenever I come over I have to take a shower after to get all the dog spit off me."

Surprised, Rhee glanced at Melody, amazed that she could be so mean, and then she saw the smile on her face and the twinkle in her eyes as she playfully punched Bonnie in the arm.

Bonnie smiled back. "Wanna sleep over this weekend?"

Melody nodded. "Beats going to the Reservation."

"Reservation? As in Indian Reservation?" Rhiannon blurted as she followed them back in to the lunchroom.

Melody arched her left brow. "You got a problem with that?"

Rhiannon blushed. "Um, no way. I think it's cool."

Turning her back, Melody muttered, "It isn't."

Bonnie shook her head and took the lead. Right over to a table that had a bunch of guys already sitting at it.

Rhiannon stopped, then waited to see what Bonnie and Melody would do.

Melody tapped one guy on the shoulder. "Scoot over, lard butt. You better not have touched my French fries."

Rhiannon blinked as the skinniest kid she'd ever seen scooched to make way for Melody, who was also tall and slim.

Bonnie giggled. "That's Peter. Dubbed Broomstick since the first grade, if you'll note his height and lack of body mass."

Rhiannon blinked and Peter waved.

Next to him was a chubby guy with dark brown hair. He looked up, grinned and popped a hot dog in his mouth, whole.

"Gross!" Rhiannon said without thinking. The rest of the kids laughed and Bonnie said, "Meet Meat, so called for the obvious reasons. Across from him is Corey."

Corey smiled. "Hey, baby, what's shakin'?"

Rhiannon smiled back. Corey was all right, with sandy blond hair and brown eyes. A few zits, but not bad.

Bonnie said, "His deal is he sucks at sports. And in Crystal Lake, sports are everything."

"I'm a chess man." Corey leered and wiggled his eyebrows in a bad Groucho Marx imitation.

Melody said, "And he thinks he's funny. *Not.*"

"I'm Rhiannon. Nice to meet you." Man, she was really doing this. She was in school, she had just been humiliated and still these guys were being cool. To her. She looked around the lunchroom, sure that everyone would be staring.

Laughing their heads off.

They weren't.

The lunchroom was loud, chaos personified. Kids were eating, talking, and pretty much not noticing the fact that Rhiannon Godfrey was even alive.

She couldn't believe her luck.

Corey leaned back. "You sure you want to sit here?"

Rhiannon stilled. Was he gonna tell her to get lost? "Yeah. Why not?"

"This is the Loser table, baby."

Meat and Broomstick gave each other high fives as they all erupted into laughter. "Yeah! Freaks and geeks!" the guys cheered.

"Geeks and freaks!" the girls giggled.

Hope blossomed in the pit of her stomach, racing like fire through her body as Rhiannon sat down between Bonnie and Corey, confident for the first time all day. "You'll never meet a bigger freak than me."

Chapter Eleven

"Well, how was it?"

"Fine, Mom. I survived."

Starla reached back from the front passenger seat, grabbed Rhee's hand and squeezed. "I knew you would, honey. I've been praying for you all day."

Rhiannon didn't share the lunchroom incident with her parents, who were so happy to see her it was kind of sad.

"I made some friends." She wouldn't mention that they were all members of the Loser Club.

"Wonderful!"

Her dad nodded, rubbing his goatee as he drove with the other hand. "How could anybody not like you, Rhee? You're fun, intelligent, beautiful, blessed..."

Rhiannon rolled her eyes and got out of the minivan the second it pulled to a stop in front of the farmhouse. "Whatever. I have homework, so I'll be upstairs." Where she could relive her day in the peace of her own room.

"Want me to bring up a snack?"

"Nah, not yet."

"Okay. Oh, I found some stuff in the laundry room; I think you must have found it in the barn? Anyway, I put it all on your bed."

She'd completely forgotten about her treasures! Well, new clothes were way more important than an old jewelry box, which was probably empty anyway.

"Thanks."

Rhee ran up the stairs to her room, opened the door and flung her backpack on the floor. She took a quick mental inventory of the room to ensure she was really alone and then looked at the bed. There they were, three beaten, old and dirty items that she'd pulled from the storage barn.

"What was I thinking?"

Ignoring the items, she sat down before the computer and logged on. Tanya had to be back already.

She wasn't on IM, so Rhee typed in a fast email.

Survived my first day. Barely. Made a new enemy, who happens to be the most popular girl at school. I made a few friends.

She paused and lifted her fingers from the keyboard. She was kind of embarrassed that the only kids who liked her were losers.

Melody is cool, I guess she lives on an Indian Reservation. How was England? I can't wait to talk to you, call me when you can.

She was going to sign off when Matthew logged on. His instant message icon popped up.

Matthew: *How was school?*

Rhiannon bit her bottom lip. So what if the jerk remembered that today had been the first day of school and she'd been dreading it to no end. It didn't mean anything. She didn't answer at first, still a little mad at him for not believing she could handle the ghost on her own.

Matthew: *Don't stay mad, Rhiannon. I've kept your secret, even though I'm worried about u.*

She really missed him, so she relented and answered.

Rhiannon: *I'm fine. No sign of the ghost.*

Rhee wasn't going to tell him anything new. She'd keep him out of the loop, just to make him feel really bad when she came back to the institute and talked about how she'd sent the ghost to the other side. *All by herself.*

Matthew: *Was it as bad as you thought?*

She glanced at her backpack, which had Melody and Bonnie's phone numbers in the front pocket. "No," she typed. "Not so bad."

Matthew: ☹ *Don't forget about us*

Rhiannon: *No way, I could never forget you guys, never. Ever.*

No matter how mad she was, Matthew was still, well,

Matthew. Her friend.

Matthew: *Call if you need to, or if you just miss me, okay?*

She exhaled and decided to forgive him.

Rhiannon: *Okay*

They caught up on institute gossip, then Rhiannon told him she had homework to do—but what she really wanted was to look at the stuff from the barn.

She logged off, wondering why he was being so great. He hadn't been that caring when she'd been at the institute. When she'd had the worst possible crush on him. And now that she'd decided she liked Jared, Matthew was being cool.

Go figure.

She sat on the edge of her bed and picked up the jewelry box. The ballerina was missing a foot. Rhee tried to open the lid, but it wouldn't budge.

She looked for a lock, but couldn't find one, so she used her mind, envisioning what she wanted to happen. The lid slowly opened, and a sad song played. Inside was a cracked mirror glued to the top of the lid and—Rhiannon's eyes widened—jewelry!

Her heart pumped hard in her chest as she drew out a string of beads. Pearls? They couldn't be real. Who would toss away real jewelry in a falling-down outbuilding?

She pulled open the drawer, not sure what to expect. An emerald green pin in the shape of a frog twinkled at her. She picked it up and played with the jewel's sparkle in the light.

Rhee was so involved with her treasures that she gasped aloud when a voice said, *"Do you like that, Rhiannon? It was mine."*

She dropped the pin, startled but not scared. "Uh, Suzanne?"

A breeze wafted playfully through her room. *"Yes."*

"Where have you been?"

"Here and there."

Rhiannon closed the lid to the jewelry box, cutting off the sad song.

"Why did you do that? I haven't heard my music box in a very long time."

Chills rose on her arms and she picked up the old Sears catalogue, the one that had the year 1900 stamped on it.

"Was this yours too?"

"Yes."

Rhiannon let it go with a thud to the ground. Her voice was higher than normal when she said, "Do you realize that you are over a hundred years old? I mean, dead?"

The breeze stilled. *"Has it been so long?"*

"Sheesh. Why haven't you crossed over?"

"I told you that I cannot leave, Rhiannon."

She scooted up the bed, until her head was resting against the wall. "Okay. But why?"

"I don't want to talk about that." A gust of air knocked the hatbox over. *"There are answers to be had, Rhiannon."*

Rhee looked over at the closet. "I couldn't find anything in there about you."

Laughter and a hint of cinnamon floated around her. *"You didn't keep your eyes open. I told you."*

Confused, Rhiannon reached for the hatbox. She carefully pulled on the old rose-colored ribbon, untying the knot. She could feel Suzanne practically breathing down her neck.

"I guess this was yours too."

"Yes."

Something about the box whispered of secrets, of cherished memories. Rhiannon was scared, but she knew that she might come closer to finding out who Suzanne was and what had happened to her if she opened it.

Since Suzanne liked to talk in riddles and wouldn't answer a straightforward question.

She hesitated over opening the box. A sense of foreboding seemed to hover around her and she didn't like it. "I'm not afraid," she lied.

The box wavered in her hands and Rhee tightened her hold. She felt a stomach-punch kind of jolt, and then she was falling. It was dark and cold and she was hurtling through time, seeing her memories mixed with another's, all too fast to sort out and examine. She was free falling and all she could do was cling to the box with both hands.

Rhee landed in the past with a thud, the hatbox still in her grip. Rhiannon felt trapped inside another person's body, and that person was saying, *"Surprise! Happy birthday, Mum. A perky Easter Bonnet, to celebrate our Lord and Savior. I don't mind saying, I was much afraid that there wouldn't be a church in this backwoods place. Here, try it on. Won't you be the prettiest mother there?"*

The young woman's mother took the hat from her daughter's hands. *"Pin it back a bit, Suzanne, you know how I hate the brow forward like that. There, do I look smart, then? Will I make your father proud?"*

"Aye! And me too..." the young woman kissed the older

woman's cheek, and Rhee could feel the papery skin beneath her own lips. She saw, *understood*, that the older woman was very ill.

The scene shimmered and changed.

They were at a funeral. Suzanne's grief surged through her own heart; Suzanne's tears fell down her own cheeks. She saw her black-gloved hand reach out to an older gentleman. *"We'll do fine, Father. I won't let you down."*

Again the scene changed, and Rhee's deep sorrow was replaced by a sharp terror. Soul-freezing fear that could only belong to Suzanne. *Why?*

Rhee's heart raced and she pressed her hand to her chest, the crazy rise and fall of her breath both reassured her and scared her, but she couldn't escape Suzanne's memories.

She blinked, water clung to her lashes and Rhiannon could see nothing but gray mist all around. Her feet were cold. She looked down, and her thin slippers were soaked through. Not hers, but Suzanne's.

The wind whipped the hem of her dress against her calves, feeling like dozens of bee stings at once. *"No!"* She shouted, not knowing why—she was in danger, Adam was *dead*, she thought wildly, and then a sharp pain exploded in her shoulder and she fell back, back into cold water that came over her head. *Danger!* Panic took over and Rhiannon tossed her hands in the air, flailing wildly as she struggled to get free. Coughing, she gulped in deep breaths of air that tasted like lake.

It was the loud smack of the hatbox flying from her hands, crashing into her stereo, that brought her abruptly out of the vision.

The simple act of breathing hurt her sore lungs. "What happened?" Her voice sounded like her own; at least that was something. Her legs trembled, and she looked down, certain that her feet would be wet.

They were dry.

Her chest constricted and she swallowed hard past a throat that felt raw, like the time she'd gotten strep throat and had to stay in bed for a week.

"Suzanne?" Her voice was a croak. She reached out with her mind, but she knew already that the spirit wasn't there.

She eyed the tipped over hatbox as if it were a poisonous snake. "Dang. That was sooo real."

Rhiannon licked her dry lips and slowed her brain down enough that she could think coherently.

"I really felt what she felt. I saw what she did. Who was Adam?" She closed her eyes, more confused now than ever before. "Blessed be the Goddess," Rhiannon said under her breath. "Show me the way." Nothing like a near-death experience to bring you closer to the Divine, she thought with chattering teeth.

"Okay. Logic. Prioritize." She touched the warm pendant against her chest and envisioned calm, a trick her mom had taught her when she was really little. Calm looked like fluffy white clouds in a pale blue sky. "I picked up the hatbox. I was able to channel a memory from Suzanne by touching something that belonged to her. What is that called?" She frowned and bit her lip while she concentrated.

"Psy—tel—no." Opening her eyes, it came to her and she snapped her fingers. "Psychometry."

Wow, she thought with a shiver. Matthew would love to be able to do this—why couldn't it have happened to him? No way, don't go there. It had happened to her, and she would deal with it just fine, thank you.

Besides, thinking that way was negative. One thing the

Institute of Parapsychology and her Wiccan mother agreed on was that negativity drew more negativity, which was dangerous.

She quickly imagined pink fluffy cupcakes of positive thoughts, another one of her mom's old tricks to chase away bad thoughts. Rhiannon had stopped using those tricks when she learned about science. *Pink fluffy cupcakes of positive thought weren't real.* Parapsychological research, lab experiments, fieldwork—that was real. Tangible in a world that was mostly chaos. For a five-year-old little girl, it was better to believe in science, which gave her some control, rather than magick, which by its definition, defied logic.

She'd need to document what had just happened.

"Suzanne wanted me to know what her past was like. Was she able to get inside my body?" That didn't feel right. So how—

Her door was thrown open and her mom yelled, panting from running up the stairs, "What happened? By the Maiden, the Mother and the Crone, I know you called for me, Rhiannon Selene. You were in danger!"

Rhee jumped to her feet, her concentration blown out the window. *Think.* Her mother couldn't know about the ghost! "Uh. I fell asleep. I had a nightmare. I was drowning." Which was sorta true.

Starla looked around the room, noticed the hatbox on its side, and looked back at her daughter.

"I must have kicked it off the bed. Is that what you heard?"

Her mom's lips pressed into a straight line across her face. "Are you all right now?"

Rhee held her hands out. They were shaking as hard as the time she'd drank two vanilla Grande latte's in a row.

"I...mmm, I think so. It was scary, Mom."

Her mom sighed and patted her chest. "I can only imagine;

Rhiannon, I was terrified. Come downstairs now and have some warm milk. Nothing is as soothing as warm milk after a nightmare."

Rhiannon scrunched up her nose at the thought of milk, warm or otherwise. Janet had kind of ruined milk for her, *at least for a while.*

"Chamomile? Okay, we can have tea instead. Chamomile is nice and calming, restful."

Rhiannon followed her mom out of her room, shutting the door firmly behind her.

One thing for sure—she was not touching that hatbox ever again!

Chapter Twelve

She'd been too scared the night before to do anything more than shove the dumb box under her bed, using the handle of her umbrella so she wouldn't touch the vibrant thing by accident. Rhee decided that time travel wasn't for her.

However, all during math class, when she wasn't watching Jared, or passing notes with Bonnie, she'd done nothing but think about it.

She kinda owed it to Suzanne to see what was inside the box. And why hadn't the jewelry affected her the same way the box had? More questions that she doubted Suzanne would bother answering.

This time when the bell rang for lunch, she wasn't worried over anything except staying clear of Janet. She'd even packed her own cheese sandwich and juice so she wouldn't have to stand in line like an open target at the duck-shooting range.

Melody was already there, sitting next to Broomstick and Meat. Corey grinned like an idiot and said, "Hey, baby. I saved you a seat by me. Wanna go steady?"

Rhiannon laughed. "I think I'll pass. Thanks."

Meat grabbed her brown paper sack. "Whatcha got in there?"

"Hey," Rhiannon said. "Give that back, I'm starving."

"Where's your food?" He pulled out her cheese sandwich and banana. "You don't have any meat in here."

"I'm a vegetarian."

The table went quiet.

"Must be how you keep your figure," Corey finally said with kissy lips.

Rhiannon tried to laugh. Corey was such a character. What would the rest of the group think? Why should it matter?

"Isn't that hard?" Melody finally asked.

"Uh, no." *Were they gonna make her sit at a different table? Was she too weird even for the losers?*

"So you don't eat Meat at *all*?" Meat's face was study of confusion.

Rhiannon grabbed her bag back. "Listen, you eat what you like, and I'll eat what I like."

Broomstick swallowed and Rhiannon watched his Adam's apple bob painfully in his throat. He asked, "Have you ever even tasted a hamburger? A juicy steak?"

"Nope. Well, we eat veggie burgers. They're good."

Meat made gagging noises. "I'd starve. I'd whittle away to nothing. I'd blow away on the first wind."

Broomstick looked at him and grinned. "Might wanna try it."

Melody giggled and shook her head. "Mean!"

Bonnie showed up, huffing, and tried to slide onto the bench next to her without looking at anybody. She dropped her lunch, which landed on Meat's tray and flipped his fries to the table.

Then she burst into tears.

Meat said, "Hey, don't worry about the fries, they're still

good." He shoved one in his mouth and chewed, showing her he wasn't mad.

Rhiannon could see that Bonnie had probably been crying before she'd dumped Meat's fries. "What's the matter?"

"N-nothing."

Rhee wasn't sure what to do, but sensed the upset that Bonnie felt. The sadness, the loneliness, and the underlying line of anger made Bonnie's aura a pulsing cobalt blue. "Something happened, Bon, and you really helped me yesterday. Let me help you."

Rhiannon knew she wasn't supposed to use her powers, but she sent thoughts of caring toward her new friend.

Making a big production out of opening her lunch bag, Bonnie muttered, "Just Janet. No big deal. I bumped into her in the hall, accidentally, and she pushed me. Called me a fat cow."

Melody yelled, "You aren't fat!"

Bonnie blinked furiously behind her glasses.

Rhiannon's hand curled around her can of juice. *Enough already.* She'd make Janet pay, and do it in a way that she wouldn't get caught. She'd do it for Bonnie too. How come Janet was so rotten? Her temper rose.

So did the can beneath her hand. She quickly slammed it down, but not before Melody looked at her funny.

Corey teased, "Hey, Bonnie, tomorrow we can walk to lunch together. You have science, right across the hall from me. I've got French. The language of looove."

Rhiannon ducked her head and ate her sandwich. It was only a matter of time now before Melody and the others realized what she was. Had anybody else seen the rising juice? It didn't matter. Melody would tell Bonnie, who would tell Corey, who would...

"I have P.E. after lunch," Broomstick said.

"So do I," Melody interrupted. "And Rhiannon does too."

A group. Rhiannon was part of a group, and there was safety in numbers. At least until her own group made her an outcast. She liked having friends, she liked it enough that she was going to try even harder to control her stupid psychic junk.

At the institute she, Tanya, and Matthew had all thought that their gifts had made them special. And there, they had. It was only in the real world that the stuff they could do got them into trouble.

Poor Matthew, he had it worse. He was a fire-starter, and all he wanted to be was a ghost hunter.

Tanya was just cool. She was the best at blending in the *everyday*. She went to a private school in the mornings, and then joined Rhiannon and Matthew at the institute in the afternoons. She could read the future by studying someone's handwriting.

A sharp pain of homesickness hit her hard.

"Woohoo, earth to Rhiannon, gothic goddess, woohoo."

Rhiannon blinked, checked her surroundings, and focused on Corey. "Don't call me that."

His eyebrow shot up. "Gothic? You dress head to toe in black."

She couldn't—no, make that wouldn't—open her big mouth and make a big deal of being called a goddess. Having them all find out she was a vegetarian was enough for one day, without adding in tidbits of her Wiccan background. Maybe Melody hadn't noticed the can floating up in the air.

She wasn't that lucky.

The bell rang and they all got up to throw away their trash and head to the next class.

She, Melody, and Broomstick walked down the hall together, but Melody was talking to Broomstick, and pointedly ignoring her.

Yeah, Rhee thought, *Melody saw it, and now she's trying to figure out how to tell everybody Rhiannon is a super freak. Man, oh man.* Her stomach flipped. Should she mention it first, or wait for Melody to make her move?

She didn't have to worry, since Melody pretty much gave her the cold shoulder. Rhiannon wished she knew what to do. What was the etiquette for revealing psychic abilities?

She knew, from past painful experience, that letting people know what she could do would only hurt her in the end.

She watched Melody stomp into the gym, her body sending off waves of irritation.

Melody plopped down on the bleachers, and Rhiannon sat next to her. She licked her lips, nervous, trying to think of a way to explain away the rising can. "Listen—"

"No." Melody turned, her brown eyes narrowed into slits. "You listen. If you don't want to be Bonnie's friend, then don't sit with us. You didn't say one word to her after she told you what happened with Janet. She trusted you enough to tell you, and then you just ignored her."

Rhiannon sat back, her hands clammy. Melody hadn't seen the can at all! Then she realized what Melody *was* saying. "Hey, what are you talking about? I like Bonnie; I like everyone at the table."

"You flirt with Corey, when Bonnie's had a crush on him since seventh grade. You act like you think you're better than we are. Well, you aren't."

Tears sprang to Rhiannon's eyes. "I don't think that. And I wasn't flirting! I had no idea that Bonnie liked him. Corey's funny, and, well, not my type. I guess I was too busy thinking about a way to get revenge on Janet that I must not have said anything." *And that was the truth.*

Melody relaxed her shoulders. "Revenge?"

"Well, yeah."

"Any ideas?"

Mmm...she had plenty of those, but nothing that would keep her secret safe. "Sort of."

The gym teacher shouted with sarcasm, "If you two would stop talking, we could start class."

Rhiannon exhaled with relief when Melody smiled, and she knew they were friends again.

Thinking of all the different ways to pay Janet back made her super hungry. So after school, she grabbed some of her mom's banana nut bread and a water bottle before heading up the stairs to her room.

Would she be going against the Wiccan Rede if she used her gifts to avenge someone? *Yes.*

Suzanne was waiting for her.

"Where have you been, Rhiannon?"

"School."

"Did you find answers?"

Annoyed, Rhiannon let her backpack fall to the floor. "No, and since you just want to play games instead of answering my questions, I don't care anymore."

A rush of wind blew through the room, icy cold. Rhiannon stayed perfectly still as Suzanne tore around, ruffling her bed covers, her curtains, and her pillows.

"You must help me!"

"And how am I supposed to do that when you disappear whenever you feel like it? And I'm telling you this—if you ever take me on a trip like that down memory lane again, well, I'm calling Mrs. Edwards and she'll *make* you go to the other side!"

"I did not make you see those things, Rhiannon. You have the ability to hear me, to feel me. You saw my mother. My father."

The air grew warm, but only for a second before the spirit begged softly, *"Help me."*

"I'm trying." Rhiannon thought about the box under her bed, then reluctantly got down on her hands and knees to make sure it was still there. She concentrated hard and mentally pulled it out where she could reach it. "You promise that it wasn't you, like, invading my body, or something?"

"I don't need your body."

Rhiannon sighed, and lifted the box on her bed. She wondered if she should put up her shields. "At least part way," she said out loud.

Suzanne's essence flew around the bed, sending pillows flying in every direction. The air grew so cold that the tip of Rhiannon's nose was freezing.

"Settle down, Suzanne. I can't help you if I get frostbite."

"I'm happy. Happy for you to see me."

"I can't see you. I was in your body, in your memories." Taking a breath for courage, Rhiannon quickly jerked the lid off of the box.

Tissue, faded and pale rose, was at the top. Rhee pulled it out, halfway expecting to see the Easter bonnet that she'd seen in her vision. To her surprise, the bottom of the box was full of pictures and letters.

Suzanne tossed the tissue into the air. *"Hurry, I haven't much time."*

A letter floated up from the stack. Rhee picked it up, taking a sip of her water from her water bottle at the same time. Then she snorted the water out through her nose. "Suzanne *Roberts?* As in the Roberts family that lives down the road? That Roberts?"

A long sigh traveled through her brain and down through her body. *"Yes."*

Rhiannon hated the loneliness that came with the sigh. "Well, why didn't you go and haunt that stupid Janet instead? Hmm? You're relatives!"

The curtains went still.

"Fine. Don't answer me. I'm getting used to it."

The letters weren't in any order at all that Rhiannon could see. The silence lay heavy in the air. She shut her eyes hard, trying to remember every last detail she'd researched about getting rid of an unhappy ghost.

She opened one eye and looked around the room. There was more to it than that. Hadn't Suzanne said she *couldn't* leave the house?

So maybe that meant that she was being held here against her will. She thought about that as she ran her fingers over a gold embossed envelope. It looked like an invitation. "What's this?"

A shiver at the nape of her neck told her of Suzanne's return. *What an adventure,* she thought. *And if I do this right, it will be me going back to the institute, where I belong. All I have to do is send you, Suzanne, on to the next plane of existence. Piece of cake.* Rhiannon laughed under her breath.

She uncovered paper that was as heavy as cardstock, and

about the size of a postcard.

"Mr. and Mrs. Miller are pleased to announce the wedding of their son, Adam Miller, to Miss Suzanne Roberts. Hmm, you were going to get married, Suzanne?"

A cold thrust of frigid air tore through the center of the room, knocking all of her knick-knacks off her table and on to the floor. Rhee clutched the invitation to her chest—the puffs of air she expelled looked like marshmallows in the instantly freezing room.

"Geez, Suzanne. Did you ever get into trouble for your temper? I'm constantly getting ragged for mine."

The whirlwind lasted a few moments longer before finally subsiding. Rhee felt like she was dealing with a kid in the middle of a tantrum. "Get a grip, so I can finish this letter. I take it you never actually got married?" It was difficult to picture Suz as a bride, solid and happy, instead of paranormally annoyed.

"No."

Shivering a little, Rhee asked, "Did you die before the wedding?"

"There was no wedding."

Rhiannon sighed. "Way to not answer my question. What happened to your fiancé?"

"Adam."

At the mention of his name, Rhiannon's body clenched with apprehension. She remembered the pain in her shoulder, the water, the suffocating, not being able to breathe, *Adam.*

Rhiannon drank the rest of her water in one long gulp. "He drowned. You met him at night, a stormy night, and he drowned. But you...you were in the water too." At the memory, Rhiannon could still taste lake water in the back of her throat.

Suzanne grew agitated, but didn't say anything.

"Crystal Lake?" Rhee guessed, "Were you on a boat? And the storm came in while you were on the water, so you lost track of time."

"NOOOOO!"

Rhiannon's hair stood on end. The spirit's scream had been filled with pain and fury, her anger bounced off the walls like a ping-pong ball gone wild.

And just like that, Suzanne was gone.

But *it* was back.

The dark foreboding presence of the thing in the closet pulsed in the room. Why did she never get a decent warning before it showed up?

Rhiannon's head pounded like there was someone with a tiny hammer right above her left eyebrow. She felt the energy being sucked out of her body. "Ouch, stop."

Using her psychic shields, she tried to defend herself against the invasion. It was too late. The invitation was ripped from her hands and thrown across the room, the hatbox was tossed to the floor, and the tissue was shredded before her eyes.

With every last ounce of telepathic energy she opened her mind and screamed, *"Mom! Help!"*

Chapter Thirteen

"I think you should stay home today."

"My third day of school and you want me to skip it? Geez, Mom." It was funny how much she was actually looking forward to seeing Melody and Bonnie. And Jared.

"Your dad and I were wondering if this has all been too much for you. We moved. We took you away from Dr. Richards and your friends. It's obvious school is traumatic for you. Nightmares all the time! I don't understand."

"We are very serious, here, Rhee." Her dad stood with his hands across his chest; his gaze was solemn. "You fainted. Again. You said that you had another nightmare. Which means that you are trying hard to bury something in your subconscious. You know you can talk to us. Are you being bullied?"

"I won't have you being picked on, not to the point that you are sick with worry when you get home!" Her mom's normally smiling face was set in concern. Even her bracelets were quiet.

"I want to go to school. Nothing is happening there that I can't handle." *Yet.*

Her dad cleared his throat. "Would you like to talk to Dr. Richards? We could make you an appointment. This is Friday. We can fly over tomorrow. I'm sure that he'd squeeze you in."

The idea of seeing Matthew and Tanya almost had her lying through her teeth. It would be so easy to tell her mom and dad that she was terrified of school, that she didn't belong, that she would never fit in.

But then who would help Suzanne? And pay back Janet? Priorities first, and then maybe she'd play up the bully card so that she could go back to the Institute. She'd be practically a hero for having solved Suzanne's mystery and sending her on to the light.

"I'm fine."

Her mom's eyebrows rose. "Well. I don't know how to help you if you won't talk to me."

"You came for me when I called. I needed that."

"You were passed out on the floor! You scared ten years off the wheel of my life, Rhiannon."

Her mom's chin trembled, so Rhee gave her a hug. "Don't worry. Once I get used to the routine of school I'm sure things will settle down."

"How about moving back to the guest bedroom? Then you'll be on the same floor as we are."

Her dad nodded. "That may be a good idea."

"No!" She had to be where Suzanne could reach her, and the old attic was the best spot. Even with that scary thing, she had an idea that Suzanne was tied to that area in some way. "I like my room." *In the daytime.*

Her parents looked at one another, and then at her. "Okay," her dad said. "But if things get worse, we will have to make a change."

Rhiannon tossed her hair over her shoulder. "I'm sick of change."

The ride to school was quiet, and Rhiannon thought about

the gut-wrenching horror she'd felt the night before. She just knew that Suzanne was being held captive in the house by that dark, evil spirit-thing in the closet.

But how to get rid of it? The smudging ritual hadn't worked, probably because she hadn't done it right. Burning a bundle of herbs, chanting and waving the smoke in the air had made her feel kinda dumb.

She felt that way often enough without the whole magick thing making it worse. Her IQ was off the charts, but her magickal abilities were right down at the bottom of the ladder with her social skills. Her mom was going to try a purifying ritual while she was at school today, to banish the nightmares. Rhee sort of wished she could tell her mom about the ghost, but she'd kept it a secret for so long she'd be better off just telling them when it was all over.

Not that Rhiannon believed in magick, anyway, but it did make her feel a little better to know that her mom, who believed in the Goddess with all her heart, was sending positive energies into the attic. Any kind of help she could get was better than nothing.

She hoped it would be enough. That dark thing was powerful. Possibly too powerful for her to get rid of on her own.

Man, if only Tanya were here. Two psychics were much more powerful than one.

She bit her lower lip. Why not see if Tanya could come here?

That would solve the problem! She tried sending the idea telepathically to her mom. *Tanya here. Tanya here.*

"Wanna beer? Rhiannon, I swear upon my sacred chalice that if I find out you are drinking, I will... I will..."

Rhiannon rolled her eyes. So much for letting her mom think it was her own idea. She said slowly and plainly, "I was thinking about Tanya being here."

"Oh. Okay." Her mom looked at her dad, who was driving. "Miles?"

Her dad looked at her in the rearview mirror. "Would that help, do you think?"

Rhee lowered her eyes, not wanting to *totally* take advantage of the fact her parents wanted her to be happy. "I miss her, that's all."

"Well, we can think it over this weekend. I don't see why not, if it's okay with her mom. And if you have your homework done." Starla winked.

"Yes!" Rhiannon felt the weight of worry slide off her shoulders as her dad pulled up to the curb. Rhiannon got out, smiling so hard it hurt her face. "Thanks!"

"Merry meet, merry part, and merry meet again, daughter mine," her mom called out the window.

They pulled away and Rhiannon heard laughter behind her. She turned, not the least bit surprised to see Janet and her flunkies crowded together as if the three of them were joined at the hip.

"Nice van—Celestial Beginnings. Is that a witch place?"

Rhiannon didn't like Janet's smirk. The power rose suddenly within her; angry. Sarcasm spewed from between her lips, and she didn't care whose feelings she hurt. "You guys get a group discount at the hairdresser? Three for the price of one?"

Janet's hand flew to her hair. The other two stared at each other and blushed.

Rhiannon snorted. "Thought so."

Janet narrowed her eyes. "How you liking school? I see you found the perfect group of friends. Losers. Just like you."

Rhiannon swallowed the rage that was lodged in her throat.

It was hard and foreign, stuck like a bitter pill. She tilted her head to the side and raised one brow high. "I chose the coolest people in this burg to hang out with—trust me, you didn't even make the short list."

Janet stepped forward with narrowed green eyes and Rhiannon met her halfway, so furious that she could taste it. It tasted a little like lake water. *I could punch her on her perfect little nose, maybe slap her cheek so hard I could see my fingerprints, or...*she brought up her hand in a fist and gasped when she saw a strange black essence surrounding her fingers like smoke. *Evil and dark. Menacing and hungry.* Wrong.

Wrong. Rhiannon stopped and stuffed her hand in her pocket, afraid of what she'd been about to do. She'd never been so instantly mad, not even at Maddie Johnson.

Janet laughed. She looked at the crowd of people that surrounded them and played it up. "That's what I thought, Brianna. You don't have the guts."

Rhiannon just stood there feeling sick to her stomach as Janet walked away with her friends.

Backing down from Janet had been the smartest thing to do. Since when had her aura turned black? Yeah, she had a temper, and yeah, she lost control, but never, ever had she felt like she could rip someone's head off.

A hand dropped on her shoulder and she squeaked.

"What was that all about?"

That voice. Kinda deep, kinda throaty. She didn't want to meet his eyes, but she forced herself.

"Ask your sister."

"I'll tell her to leave you alone."

Great, so now he thought she was a total wuss who couldn't take care of herself? *Perfect.* She swung her backpack over shoulder. "Don't worry about me. Janet's the one who would've been hurt."

Stupid guy just had to laugh. "I don't know about that." He shrugged. "Me and my older brother, Brian, have always rough-housed with her. She can hang in there. Mean left-hook." Jared grinned and threw a punch in the air.

Rhiannon felt her lips twitch as her mood lightened. "Thanks for the warning, Rambo."

His eyes widened. "You like those old Sylvester Stallone movies? I love 'em!"

She smiled cautiously, wondering why he was being nice to her. "Tango and Cash?"

"Classic."

"I like a lot of the old movies, especially the horror movies."

"The really old ones, like Dracula with, what's his name? Boris? Bella?"

Rhiannon laughed. "Something like that." The anger had drained out of her, and the more she talked and laughed with Jared, the better she felt. When would he remember he was talking to a member of the Loser Club?

Rhiannon hadn't realized that they'd been walking and talking all the way to math class. She hesitated just outside. Would he go in the door and sit with his friends, pretending that they hadn't just been having a blast?

Or would he walk in with her and show everyone they were having fun?

"Oh, great comeback, by the way. Choosing the coolest people in the school. I think I may have been insulted, since you don't talk to me."

"I'm talking to you right now," Rhiannon pointed out. They were through the door. His friends were looking at him. Caleb even smiled.

"So now I'm 'Rhiannon Godfrey cool'. Good to know." He gave her a grin that had her floating all the way back to her seat.

Bonnie poked her in the arm with a pencil. "Are you nuts? First you almost drop the gloves with Janet, and then you're flirting with Jared? Her twin brother?"

"How could you have heard about that already? It just happened!"

"Word travels fast; most people have cell phones." Bonnie sat back and picked at her fingernails. "Do you have one?"

Knowing that this was a sore spot for Bonnie, Rhiannon was tempted to lie. "Uh, well. For emergencies and stuff."

Bonnie pushed her glasses up the bridge of her nose. "I guess you're allowed to go to the movies, too, on a Friday night and stay out until past seven without a chaperone."

Bonnie sighed so deeply that Rhiannon blurted, "Hey. How about a sleep over? At my house?"

Bonnie blinked owlishly behind her lenses. "Me?"

"Yeah, we can ask Melody too. I mean, I don't think I can do it tonight." She had a ghost to dispel first. "But maybe tomorrow." *Maybe, Rhiannon, you should keep your mouth shut. How are you going to explain your parents? Let alone a few ghosts?*

But Bonnie looked so happy, Rhiannon couldn't take the invitation back. She just kept on going, like that pink battery bunny. "And we can do make-up, and nails, and I have this awesome eyebrow waxing kit. It'll be fun!"

Now she just had to figure out how to get the ghosts out of her house before Saturday night.

By lunch, everyone had heard about the confrontation

she'd had with Janet. Meat stood up and started pumping a victory fist in the air when he saw her.

"Way to go! Heard you faced the beast today."

Rhiannon could feel her eyes widen. "Uh. Dang. What else did you hear?"

Corey grinned. "Baby doll, you are a-okay in my book. I hear you dished some of Janet's crap right back to her. I like a chick with guts."

Broomstick's Adam's apple did that bobbing thing. "Yeah. That took guts, all right. I've been avoiding Janet Roberts since second grade."

Rhiannon sank down to her seat. "Guys, it was nothing, really. Especially since I backed down." Which was more and more humiliating the more people congratulated her for standing up to Janet in the first place. But she hadn't recognized the anger that had been inside her. Or maybe she had recognized it, and knew it was...bad.

No matter what else, that blackness had been scary. Ten times worse than anything she'd ever felt before.

Bonnie said, "I don't care if you did back down. What I heard was that it looked like you would have popped her, right up until *you* decided to change your mind."

"I think you'd be the first girl ever expelled from Crystal High for brawling." Meat grinned.

"Do you see why I'm in love with you, Rhiannon?"

Bonnie sucked in a breath and Melody gave Rhiannon a pointed look.

Rhiannon smacked Corey's arm. "If I thought for one second that you were serious, I'd have to deck you. But since we're *just friends*, it's all good."

Could she be any clearer?

Melody smiled. "Ha. She called you on that one, Corey boy."

He put a hand over his heart. "I'm wounded. And here I thought my extreme good looks would have you falling senseless at my feet."

Bonnie nodded and Rhiannon elbowed her while saying, "Your feet are huge, and they probably smell. Anybody have an extra spoon? I forgot mine."

Reaching into her oversized lunch bag, Bonnie said, "Here. Napkin? Hey, Melody, Rhiannon's invited us to sleep over Saturday night."

Rhiannon took the spoon, declined the napkin, and waited for Melody to laugh her head off.

Instead, Melody said, "But I thought we were staying at your house. My mom already said I could go, and since she has to work late, she won't have time to meet Rhiannon's parents before then, so I know she'll say no. How about Rhiannon comes to your house too?"

Rhiannon held her breath. She had never slept away, like at a slumber party, ever. Plenty of hotel rooms, which got old after a while, despite room service. What would Bonnie say? She ate her pudding like she didn't care one way or the other.

Bonnie smacked her forehead, "Oh, yeah! Sorry, Melody. I'm sure my mom will say yes, Rhiannon. She loves to meet my new friends. Gives her an excuse to cook even more food."

The boys all added their two cents in for what a slumber party should be, and then they all invited themselves, period.

"I don't think so, guys. Don't you remember my tenth birthday party at the roller rink? My mom had boys on one side, girls on the other. She gave us all a lecture on sharing drinking cups or silverware. I think she actually told us we'd get cooties."

Everybody laughed, especially Rhiannon. She was off the

hook, with at least an extra week to get the ghosts out of her house.

And she'd been invited to her first sleepover.

Chapter Fourteen

Her parents were awfully talkative on the way home. "Let's have Chinese food tonight. We can celebrate your first week of school."

Rhee smiled, remembering all the stuff her mom would celebrate, just because. The loss of her first tooth had gotten her cookies with strawberry frosting. Her first hair cut had been photographed and scrapbooked. "Mom, I only went three days."

"It counts."

"I'm kind of tired though."

Her parents exchanged a secretive look and her dad said, "I'm not surprised, you haven't been sleeping well. We just have a few errands to run. You know, some of the furniture for the shop came in today. We got Betsy moved to her new home."

"Cool, does she like it?" *I hope she takes moving better than I did.*

"I put a barrel of petunias right outside the gate."

"That's nice, Mom. She can see them, smell them, and not get to them."

"If we let her do what she wants, which is eat all of the petunias, she'll get sick. This way she can have them as a treat."

Rhiannon shook her head. It was weird mom-logic.

"I hope she doesn't get too lonely. She'll be farther away from the house, and she won't be able to see us where she is now."

"She won't be lonely," her mom said, and started humming under her breath.

After an hour, Rhiannon couldn't hold back a yawn. "Can we please go home yet?"

"We still have to pick up the Chinese." Her dad glanced at his watch. "We'll be just in time."

Rhiannon sat up, suddenly wide awake. Just in time? Hope rose from her toes to her brain. Did they have Tanya fly in this afternoon? Yes! She would gladly give up spending the night over at Bonnie's in order to spend the weekend with Tanya.

She tried not to let them know she was in on their surprise, but it was so hard to sit still. She hadn't seen her friend in a month. She wouldn't even bother asking if she could go to Bonnie's now...

Yes, yes, yes, she thought to herself as they drove up to their farmhouse.

No, no, no. No cab. No sign of company. Her shoulders sagged with disappointment and she opened the van door.

"Leave the bags for now, Rhee. We have a surprise for you!"

Her dad was shuffling his feet like he had to go to the bathroom. Why was he so excited? She sure as heck didn't see Tanya anywhere. "This isn't about Mom's furniture, is it?"

Strange, but knowing her parents, possible.

Her mom clapped her hands. "Hurry on back."

Rhee called herself all kinds of names for thinking even for a second that they'd brought her friend all the way from Vegas just to get her out of the dumps. She straightened her shoulders, determined to be mature and pleasant as she oohed and aahed over her mom's new stuff.

They rounded the corner of the house and Rhiannon looked to the barn, but the sun was in her eyes and she couldn't see very well.

"Is that Betsy in the corral? I thought you said you'd put her in her new home."

Then she heard the sound of neighing. Since when did Betsy do horse impressions?

She blinked, wiped her eyes and stumbled to a halt. "Crap! Is that a horse?"

"Language!" her mom reprimanded without any real heat.

"Sorry." She glanced at her dad, who was also staring at the horse.

A horse. For her. *I can't believe this is happening to me!* "All she needs is a horn sticking from her forehead to be a unicorn! She's so beautiful."

Her parents laughed. "I remember when you used to believe in magick, Rhee," her mom said softly. "I'm hoping that you'll find room in your heart to believe again."

Rhiannon didn't even think to roll her eyes. She walked toward the gorgeous animal, all white and wonderful and still. The horse met her gaze as candidly as any human, and Rhiannon felt the instant connection between them as if it were tangible.

Then Jared stepped from behind the horse's head. "Surprised? Your parents picked her out themselves. They were very specific on your behalf. C'mon. Come give her an apple."

Rhiannon blurted, "What are you doing here?"

His smile faded. "I'm delivering the horse your parents bought for you. My family owns a horse breeding farm."

Figures, they owned everything else in Crystal Lake. Her

feet remained glued to the ground. Jared's hair glinted like gold beneath his hat. The sun was setting behind him, and he looked like he could have come from another world.

One that had unicorns.

He was holding out the apple to her as if she were the horse that needed gentling. Well, she wasn't afraid of anything.

She took a step forward. Starla laughed with sheer delight, the sound like music in the quiet air. "Are you surprised?"

Rhiannon turned back and said, "Totally. Thanks! Aren't you guys coming?"

"No. You get acquainted first. Get to know her. We love you, Rhiannon."

She blushed, with both pleasure and embarrassment.

Jared grinned, lop-sided but cute. "Not many kids get a new horse just for finishing one part of a week at school."

Rhiannon looked down at her feet. "Yeah, well. I'm special."

Jared tugged at her ponytail. "You think I don't know that?"

Rhiannon felt as if her entire body was on fire. He was looking at her like...like...like he *liked* her. And that just wasn't possible.

She looked away, taking the apple from his hands. "Does she have a name?"

"Nope. You get to do that."

"I don't know how to ride," she said as she scratched the horse's side.

"Lucky for you, your parents hired me to give you riding lessons. One on one."

She turned her head. Had his voice gotten deeper? His eyes even greener?

Is the sun totally frying my brain, or what?

"Uh... Cool?"

He took her hand and spread the fingers apart so that the apple was sitting flat in the center of her palm. "Here, like this."

Her hand was going to melt right off her arm and land with a splash on the ground. Butterflies were duking it out in her stomach and she had to fight not to pull her hand out of his.

And if she thought she'd had a crush on Matthew, then what, the Goddess help her, was this?

She took a deep breath and held her hand out to the horse. She would just ignore her feelings until she could deal with them.

Later.

"Hi," she said softly to the horse. "I'm Rhiannon," she told the placid mare. "And to think that before I moved here I'd never had a pet, and now I have two. I hope you like cows, but even if you didn't, you'd still like Betsy. She's a smart cow, just like you are a smart horse. Aren't you, girl?"

The horse's mouth tickled her palm; its nose was like velvet, all soft and black. Rhiannon let her sniff her skin and didn't budge when the mare's teeth gently scraped her skin to take the apple.

"Wow."

"Great, huh? You're a natural with animals."

His breath was warm against her ear and she shivered. "She's beautiful. I'm going to name her Moonstone."

Jared chuckled. "Your family sure has a way with names."

The sound of his laughter had her wondering why she had to be fourteen, and why she had to have a crush on the most popular guy in school, and most of all, why Janet had to be his sister.

"So what made you pick 'Moonstone'?"

Could she trust him enough to tell him that the moonstone was her birth crystal?

Despite his warm smile and friendly eyes, she didn't think so. "Her color, I guess."

He nodded. "Well, it's better than White Rock."

She smiled, "Or Lunar Pebble?"

He laughed. "How 'bout, mmm, Cheese Head? You know, after the man in the moon?"

She forgot to be intimidated by his looks and family name and punched him in the arm. "Completely lame, Jared. Cheese Head. Did you hear that, Moonstone? Geez."

The horse whinnied, and Rhiannon couldn't believe she was standing with Jared in front of her very own horse. Which was kinda big, now that she thought about it. She checked out the size of Moonstone's legs.

"Hey...you want to get on?"

Rhiannon's heart dropped to her heels. "Uh. As in, a saddle, and everything?" *I am going to look so completely stupid. I have never done this before. And Jared, probably born-in-the-saddle Jared, will watch my total humiliation.*

He was looking at her, waiting for her answer.

She gulped, and looked at Moonstone again. "I'll probably fall and break my neck, and then I'll have to miss school, and then..."

"I promise I'll catch you if you fall."

Rhiannon's breath caught in her throat. "How can a girl go wrong with a promise like that?"

She thought of Janet, mean, spiteful Janet. "Listen, I guess, you know, whatever happens on these lessons, it's like, confidential, right?"

He threw his head back and laughed. "In other words, no blabbing to Janet if you happen to make a mistake."

She sighed. "Yeah. Let's have a no-blab rule."

"Deal. Ready?"

"Don't I have to warm up or something?"

He shook his head sadly, but there was a light that she really, really liked in his eye. "Rhiannon, the first thing you have to do is relax."

She snorted.

"And the second thing you have to do is trust me."

She couldn't even summon up a snort for that one.

"Pretty tall orders, Jared."

She found his hands at her waist and tried to step back, but she bumped into her horse.

"Easy," he said, and Rhiannon wasn't sure which one of them he was talking to. "I'm just gonna help you." He turned her sideways, then cupped his hands together. "Step up."

"Uh, hey, I am totally afraid of heights."

"You'll be fine. Get comfortable."

"Ha! My nose is gonna start bleeding 'cause of the altitude change."

He laughed. "Hang on."

"Hang on to what?"

"The reins. That leather strap. Are you ready?"

"No. I'm not." Rhiannon tightened her knees against Moonstone's belly. The horse sent her an encouraging glance so Rhiannon swallowed and said, "Okay. Ready. Where are we going?"

Jared grinned. "Good job, a little looser on the reins...there you go. We're just gonna go around in a circle."

Rhiannon blushed. "Oh, man, so this is really like that thing at the fair? You know? Where you pay five bucks to ride a camel around and round? I always felt bad for the camel. Won't Moonstone get sick? Dizzy?"

Jared patted Rhiannon's leg. "We'll just go around twice. Let you gals get to know one another."

"Gals? Did you really just say *gals*? That is so John Wayne."

"Nothing the matter with John Wayne, is there? Or are you saying that I'm too country?"

She just might have put her foot in her mouth. She yanked it out. "I didn't say that! I like John Wayne fine. I don't know about being called a gal, is all."

He tipped his hat and said, "Sorry ma'am," in such an exaggerated drawl that Rhiannon almost fell off the horse, she was laughing so hard.

"Excellent, you could be an actor."

"Nope. Horses are for me."

"You like breeding them?"

"Yeah."

"So, you plan on staying in Crystal Lake, like, forever?"

"Sure. My great-great grandfather was the first settler in this area. He came over from England, leaving his wife and daughter behind for five years until he had the beginnings of a town. His wife was very city—" Jared peered at her from beneath the brim of his hat, "—and great-great grandpa didn't want to scare his wife and child away from their new home, you know, if it was too rustic."

So, Rhiannon thought, Jared knows his family history pretty well. Did he know what happened to Suzanne?

"How did the daughter like it here?"

"Don't think much. She ran off with her fiancé, and left great-great grandpa all alone after her mom, his first wife, died."

Rhiannon jerked her head in his direction to see if he was kidding, but he wasn't even looking at her.

"In fact, we still live in the original Roberts homestead. How many people can say that, huh?"

Rhiannon swallowed. Her mouth was too dry to speak so she let him lead her and Moonstone around one more time.

"Yeah. Cool." She bit her lip, wondering how to get more information from Jared without seeming too odd.

She exhaled, keeping her tone casual. "I suppose that you have all of his stuff? Like, set up in a room, or something?"

Jared glanced at her. "I guess we have some. Up in the attic, probably."

Rhiannon shivered in the bright sun. How could she tell people *how* she knew that the Roberts family history was wrong? Was it important, or even necessary? "I bet you have a bunch of pictures too." She'd really like to see what Suzanne looked like.

"We have some, in a book. You sound really interested. Do you know your family tree? I think it's great when you can trace it so far back." He came to a halt as they finished the ride.

Rhiannon shook her head. The pride in Jared's voice was obvious. "Nope."

He knew his history all right.

Too bad it was all a lie.

Chapter Fifteen

It was Saturday night, and she was having a blast—who knew that a sleep over could be so fun? Rhiannon wiggled her toes. "The cotton reminds me of a bunny's butt."

Melody laughed, and finished applying a coat of Dancing Apple Red to her left foot. "There!" She examined her feet, moving them this way and that. "What do you think, Bonnie?"

Bonnie grinned. "My mom will be furious that I'm not using pale pink. Rhiannon, I'm so glad that you brought all of your polishes."

"Make-up too, Bonnie. You ready for a make-over?"

Bonnie's skin turned blotchy red on top, and went a shade paler underneath. "Um, well, I've never worn make-up, and I don't know, my mom might get really mad, and..."

Melody held up a pillow from Bonnie's bed. "Enough about your *mom* already! Do you want to try? It washes off, for Pete's sake."

Rhiannon could tell that Bonnie was tempted. Very. She opened her make-up case, a gift from her mom for her fourteenth birthday, and said, "Inside this leather case we have lip glosses, guaranteed to soften your pucker. Eye shadows designed to accent what should be every woman's most mysterious feature, blusher for just that right hint of feminine color, meant to allure and capture the man of your dreams."

Melody and Bonnie cracked up and Melody said around a giggle, "What if that man is a still a boy?"

"Hey, leave Corey alone." Bonnie giggled. "He's perfect."

Rhiannon arched her brow. "Well? You wanna go for it?"

Her friend sighed. "Yeah. Just don't make me look like a, you know..."

"Hooker?" Rhiannon prodded.

Melody grabbed her stomach and laughed. "Oh, right, like Bonnie could ever look like one of those!"

Rhiannon got up, walking on her heels so her toes wouldn't get smudged. "Bonnie has great potential." She walked around her friend, who was practically cowering in her beanbag chair. "Awesome cheek bones, cat-shaped eyes, green with golden flecks. Hair needs shaping and highlights, but that is a piece of cake."

Snapping her fingers, Rhee blew out a breath. "I should have brought my scissors. Oh, well, I have those tiny cuticle scissors, they should work."

Melody asked with a mouth full of popcorn, "You always wanted to be a make-up lady?"

"Psh. Artist. Make-up *artist*. And no, this is just a hobby."

"Have you ever done this on anyone else before?" Bonnie asked quietly, her eyes large behind her frames.

"Well, sure. My friend Tanya was my first guinea pig, and she turned out great. We added purple highlights to her hair, and she let me pierce her ear."

Bonnie gulped. "No piercing!"

"I agree," Rhiannon said with a grin. "Too much blood."

Melody's gasp had Rhiannon turning her way. "Hey, wanna help? You wear a little make-up, so you know the difference between a blusher and an eye shadow, right?"

Melody tossed a pillow at Rhiannon, which hit her in the leg. "Toes! I hate having to re-do them. Well?"

The three girls shared huge grins and said in unison, "Let's do it!"

A while later, Bonnie squirmed beneath the towel that they'd draped over shoulders. "Are you done yet?"

Melody, totally into the assistant thing, whacked her on the shoulder with a blush brush. "Beauty takes time."

"And pain. This will just sting a little bit." Rhiannon warned.

"Ouch! What was that?"

Melody looked at Rhiannon. "Tweezers?"

"I forgot my eye-brow waxing kit, but I don't think she's ready for that yet anyway."

Rhiannon bit her lower lip, concentrating on making Bonnie a work of art. She glanced at Melody. "What do you think?"

"Is her nose supposed to be green?"

"What?" Bonnie squealed.

"Yes," Rhiannon replied patiently. "Green base on red skin helps tone it down. Then the cover-up goes over the top, and smoothes out everything."

"That is so cool," Melody said.

"Like you have to worry, you have naturally gorgeous skin."

"If you like brown," Melody said with a semi-snarl.

Rhiannon looked up from the eyebrow shaping procedure. "I read a lot of fashion magazines. I used to travel, tons of places. Your skin is *in*."

Melody huffed. "Not in Crystal Lake."

Rhiannon tapped the tweezers against her palm. "It's not

Crystal Lake that's bad—it's Janet Roberts. Think about it—who's the one who sets the example? I mean, I've met other nice kids at school. Well, kids who are all right, when Janet or one of her friends isn't around."

Melody stiffened. "Bonnie and I decided a long time ago that we didn't want friends like that."

Rhiannon took a mental step back at the angry look on Melody's face. "Okay. That makes sense. How long ago was that, junior high? Haven't you grown up since then? Maybe some of them have too. I mean, Crystal Lake may be a blip on the map, but it has cable. Look at the girls who are hot right now. J-Lo, Beyonce, Penelope Cruz, Queen Latifah, Shakira, Alicia Keys and the list goes on."

"Is there a point here?" Melody demanded.

"Yeah. You *are* beautiful, and you might as well let people know that you know it."

Bonnie gasped, then started giggling. "I am such a horrible friend. You always tell me I'm not fat, but I've never told you that you weren't..."

"Indian?" Melody scowled.

Bonnie shut her mouth with a snap.

Rhiannon said, "I don't see what the big deal is. People are fighting for the preservation of Indian Reservations, more and more Indians are claiming their heritage. I just hate to see you treat yours like it isn't worth being proud of."

Melody stared at her, and Bonnie peeked up at them even though she was supposed to have her eyes shut.

Rhiannon held the gaze, refusing to blink or back down. She wasn't prepared for Melody to change the subject all together.

"Whatever. Is Bonnie done yet?"

Rhiannon shrugged, not wanting to push Melody too hard. She knew very well what it felt like to have to re-examine yourself. Who you wanted to be versus who you thought you were. And then there was that little thing of how you actually behaved, which *always* messed her up.

"Powder, please?"

Melody held up the container. "Shimmering sheer?"

"Perfect!" With one last swipe across the bridge of Bonnie's nose, Melody turned Bonnie around so that she was facing the mirror. "Ready?"

Bonnie had her eyes scrunched tight. "Yeah."

Rhiannon nodded to Melody, who swept off the towel and said, "Open!"

Holding her breath, Rhee waited for Bonnie to say something...anything. But she just kept staring at herself. Melody and Rhiannon exchanged a look over the top of her head as her chin started trembling.

"Bonnie? Dang it, we can wash it right off." Melody patted her friend on the shoulder and Rhiannon felt the disappointment like a punch to the gut.

"I'm sorry, Bonnie. I just thought, well, that it would be fun. If you don't like it, I have make-up remover and—"

"Not like it? I don't even look like me!" Bonnie peered closer to the mirror and Melody handed over her glasses.

Rhiannon grinned, now that she knew the issue. "All you, only enhanced. *CosmoGIRL!* says that the majority of teens who suffer acne can calm it down just by changing what they eat."

Melody warned, "Not one word about your mom."

Bonnie nodded, too happy with her new look to go there. "I can't believe what you did to my hair; I have bangs."

"Wispy bangs, that can be blended back if you want. Now,

since you are happy with your transformation so far, how about this?" She looked at Melody and jerked her head to the left.

Melody yelled, "Closet raid!"

Bonnie said, "But I don't have anything."

Rhiannon clucked her tongue. "Everybody has something." She followed Melody to Bonnie's closet and drawers. Everything she pulled out was sizes too big. "Why do you buy this stuff?"

"My mom does."

"Well then, why does she buy it so..." Rhiannon looked at Bonnie and then held up a pair of jeans that all three of the girls could fit into. "Large?"

"You saw my mom."

Rhiannon bit her lip. Bonnie's mom was, hmm, on the plus side. She probably shopped at Woman's World. Did she just assume that Bonnie would be...er...big too?

"Your mom has a great smile. But I see your point. Have you tried talking to her about shopping in your own section?"

"Once. But she just shook her head and said we aren't made of money and she wanted to buy things that I could grow into."

Rhiannon snorted. "If you grow into these, you're gonna be in trouble. I'd hate to see your cholesterol count."

Sighing, realizing that she would have to take drastic measures to get Bonnie to see the beautiful girl she was, Rhee said, "Off with your shirt."

"What?"

"Off."

"No!" Even Bonnie's make-up couldn't hide her embarrassment.

Melody lowered her voice. "This is supposed to be fun."

Rhiannon said, "Okay, but her shirt looks like a muumuu. I can't see what she looks like underneath."

"I'm not as big as my clothes, but I'm not skinny, either."

"Skinny is overrated."

Melody said, "You are not fat." Then she nodded, understanding what Rhiannon was doing. "Take off your shirt."

"You'll still have on your bra and stuff, so don't worry. It isn't like it's gonna hurt or anything." Rhee tapped her toe against the floor.

"Don't laugh."

Rhiannon rolled her eyes. "Trust me when I tell you that I would never laugh at you. Do you know this is the first sleepover I've ever been invited to?"

Melody and Bonnie said, "No way!" at the same time.

"Yeah."

Bonnie asked sympathetically, "Too much traveling with your mom?"

Rhiannon looked away. "Right. So?"

"Okay."

Bonnie unbuttoned her extra large flannel shirt and slipped it off slowly.

"Oh, man!"

"You've been hiding that?" Melody whistled. "I can see your mom's plan. If you were to dress to fit your body, boys would be calling non-stop."

Bonnie crossed her arms over her chest.

Rhiannon ran over to her suitcase, opened it, and started rummaging. "Try this!"

"I cannot fit into your clothes," Bonnie said in disbelief.

"You are a little shorter than me, but it's a miniskirt, so it doesn't matter. Melody, wasn't there a plain white T-shirt in one of those drawers?"

By the time they got Bonnie into the T-shirt, one that her mom forbid her to wear in public, probably because it showed curves, and matched it with the denim mini and large black belt, added really cute short black cowboy boots and fluffed her hair, Bonnie was a knock-out.

"Look out, Corey," Rhiannon said.

Melody whistled again. "I can't believe it. Don't slump, Bonnie, you look amazing."

Bonnie swallowed hard and twirled in front of the mirror. "I can't believe it either. But I could never wear this to school, my mom would kill me."

"You need to talk your mom into buying you some stuff that fits, things that you like. I'd be happy to go with you." Rhiannon vowed then and there to make Bonnie throw out all her flannel shirts, unless they fit.

Melody said, "I want to go too."

"It takes money," Bonnie sensibly pointed out.

"Don't you have any?" Rhiannon couldn't imagine not having a clothes budget.

"Some, from birthdays and Christmas."

"Break out the piggy bank," Melody said.

There was a quick knock on the door, and then Bonnie's mom came in with a plate of chocolate chip cookies. The three girls stood still, caught red-handed in the act of making Bonnie beautiful.

Her mom stopped. Her mouth opened and closed and no sound came out.

Bonnie stuttered, "Uh, we were just, um, playing around."

Her mom slowly set the cookies on the dresser, still staring at her daughter as if she'd never seen her before.

Rhiannon knew she was about to be sent home with her sleeping bag.

It was worse than that.

Bonnie's mom's eyes filled with tears that made Rhiannon want to start bawling too.

Then she turned and left the girls alone without saying a single word.

Chapter Sixteen

When Darlene, Bonnie's mom, left the room, she took some of the fun and excitement with her. In a quieter mood, the girls cleaned up and settled on the floor, talking about hot guys and ways to get even with Janet until they finally drifted off to sleep. Rhee fell asleep with her pillow clutched to her chest, thinking of Jared.

She was the first to get picked up in the morning. Rhee'd asked her mom to be there by ten, just in case she wasn't having a good time.

She'd had a *great* time, but she couldn't look Bonnie's mom in the eye. She mumbled a "thank you" and ran out to the van.

"Have fun?" her mom asked.

"Yeah." Other than getting an unwanted insight into someone else's family life. "Can they sleep over next weekend?"

Her mom grinned. "Of course! We'll make popcorn and caramel apples and—"

"Mom! We'll just hang out in my room. Can I have chips and stuff?"

Starla looked over her sunglasses at her and Rhee fidgeted. "You know I don't like it when you eat that junk."

"Please?"

Her mom trained her eyes on the road. "Being a normal teen doesn't mean that you can forget about being healthy. Healthy in spirit, healthy in mind, healthy in body."

"I'm not asking for hot dogs!"

Her mom gasped. "I should hope not; the answer would definitely be no."

Rhiannon seethed, silently planning a way to bring chips and soda home from school and sneak them up to her room.

Her mom raised one eyebrow. "I caught that, Rhiannon Selene."

"Come on, Mom. I'm trying to fit in, and I can't do it if you serve applesauce and banana chips." *Please, no more muffins.*

"Puffins? What are those?"

Rhiannon looked out the window. "Oh, these gross cheese things."

"We'll see. Probably." Then she smiled. "I can't wait to meet your new friends! We got a letter in the mail from the school."

Rhiannon froze. Why? What had she done wrong?

"Did you know that Crystal Lake High School has an annual rodeo?" Her mom laughed. "Imagine crowning a prince and princess. I think you should try out for it."

Rhiannon sucked in a breath, glad that it was that kind of a letter. "I don't think so. Janet Roberts already has her eye on the freshman crown."

"Oh. Well, it said in the letter that anybody could try for it. But if you don't want to, that's fine with me. We'll have to go and buy you some clothes, though."

"Mom, I am *so* not buying anything with fringe."

Her mom snickered. "To tell you the truth, honey, I don't blame you."

She hauled her sleeping bag and suitcase up to her room, dropping them in front of the closet with a thud. Rhee hated going inside the closet, and had gotten in the habit of grabbing a few outfits at a time to keep handy.

But she was out of clean clothes since she'd given the denim miniskirt to Bonnie to keep.

She stared at the closet door. "Chicken, chicken," she called herself before quickly unlocking the door and opening it. She flipped on the light, and fought the temptation to just snatch whatever was closest.

Rhee walked to the back of the closet where her shoes were stacked on the new shelves, taking enough stuff out so she'd have clothes through Wednesday. She took a few shirts, two pairs of jeans, and some shoes. She was backing out, relieved, when she dropped a shoe from the top of the pile.

Sweat broke out on the back of her neck as she stared at it.

Get out, she thought immediately. *Get out, don't worry about the shoe. You can wear one shoe. Start a new trend.*

"Wimp," she said out loud. Gathering her self-respect, she bent down to pick up the stupid shoe and noticed that the same black essence she'd seen around her fingers the day she'd confronted Janet was seeping beneath the shelves.

It looked like spilled black paint, thick and slow and wet.

It couldn't be good. She gulped and then the closet door slammed shut behind her, locking her inside with the black aura. Rhee quickly tried to put up her shields, but they wouldn't go. Her psychic psyche was open to whatever the black thing turned out to be.

Not good, not good, she panicked.

She backed up into a row of shirts. Think, Rhiannon. How would Mrs. Edwards fight this off? Would she address it? So far, Rhiannon had been trying to block the evil, and when that didn't work, she ran from it.

Shaking, she decided to hold her ground. It was time.

"Who *are* you?" she demanded.

Black-gray smoke rose from the pool on the floor, the pool that was spreading like tentacles to touch her shoes. The ones that she was wearing.

Creepy. Her heart raced and her palms started to sweat.

Control, focus.

"Who are you?" she asked again.

The shelves shook, knocking her neatly stacked shoes to the floor. Some of them landed in the black essence, and Rhiannon knew she would never wear them again.

There was no answer, but it seemed like a cloud of evil was hovering around her. She could call for her mom, but that would just freak everybody out again.

No. She had to handle this by herself and stop being such a wimp.

She took a deep breath and stared at the black wisps that were trying to solidify. "Go back to where you came from. Go back. You are not wanted here."

Her psychic powers were gone. Somehow the black thing was able to block her abilities.

Well, she was from a Wiccan family too. She'd been reading a few spells that she could try, just in case. Chanting was supposed to work. Especially rhyming chant. Her brain wouldn't focus, so she pinched down hard on the thin skin between finger and thumb.

It cleared her head. She shut her eyes tight. "*Evil black, you must go back. Evil black, you must go back. Seek the light, escape the night, evil black, you must go back.*"

Her voice was shaky and she opened her eyes, expecting to see the essence at her toes.

It was gone.

In the blink of an eye she had the closet door open and she was outta there. If her mom wanted to know why she kept wearing the same old thing, well...she'd have to think of something.

"Rhee?"

She heard her dad calling from downstairs, so she opened her bedroom door, leaned out and yelled, "Yeah?"

"Tanya's on the phone; can you pick up in your room?"

Relief gave her some of her strength back. "Yeah! Cool, thanks, Dad." What fabulous timing—Rhee curled up in the recliner next to the large window. She needed sunlight. Lots and lots of cleansing sunlight. Whatever had been in the closet was gone. *For now.* "Tanya? What took you so long to call?"

"I just got back into Vegas yesterday, but I've been thinking about you non-stop. Are you all right? How's that ghost thing going?"

"Tanya!"

"Oops. Sorry, I'm by myself. Mom went grocery shopping. I bet you don't miss all the traveling, do you?"

"Well, no. Not as much as I thought I would."

"I'm a little jealous, I have to say."

"Jealous? You're insane. Try living here awhile, and you'll be *so* over it."

She laughed. "Your dad asked if Mom would let me come over for the weekend, maybe next weekend. But you know my mom. It is *not* happening. How the woman can function with germaphobia is beyond me."

"Can't you talk her into it?"

"I'll try, but don't hold your breath. Tell me about your ghost instead."

Rhiannon settled back in her seat, getting Tanya all caught up on the latest, including that last nasty part in the closet. "Can you believe that the rhyming chant got rid of it?"

"Not for good, and you know it. It sounds like it's getting stronger."

Rhee knew her friend was right, so she changed the subject. "Hey, you can see the future by reading handwriting...what if I were to send you something Suzanne had written? Could you help me?"

"Dunno, that would be a past thing, but we can try. Has to be the original, though. Not a copy."

Rhiannon hated to get back into the hatbox, but knew she was going to have to. The black thing was getting stronger. She was going to do another smudging ritual, or move back into the guest bedroom. She didn't like the way the black stuff made her feel. *Angry and tired. Emptied.*

"Tanya, do you think it's possible for one ghost to trap another ghost?"

"I guess it would depend on the death. Were they killed at the same time? In the same place?"

"I can't get Suzanne to answer me. She talks in circles. And that stuff in the closet is...scary."

"You never freak!"

"This is bad, I'm telling ya."

"You just say the word, and I'll have Dr. Richards over there before you can say oogly-boogly."

Rhiannon laughed and rocked in her seat. "And why would I ever say oogly-boogly?"

Tanya snickered, "Because it sounds cool."

After they hung up, Rhiannon went to the closet and locked it. Then she dragged a trunk in front of the door. And *then* she lit a purifying candle and put it on top of the trunk before going to the hated hatbox.

Using the powers of her mind, she was able to flip through the items inside without actually touching anything. She shivered and muttered, "This is just crazy. Who am I kidding?"

Maybe she really should talk to Dr. Richards.

But she was so close! If she could just figure out *why* Suzanne was stuck here, then she'd be home free. She could do this herself and get all the credit and the glory.

Rhee came across a picture. Black and white. She really wanted to pick it up and get a closer look. Was it worth getting sent wherever Suzanne's memory took her? Chewing her bottom lip, she settled for putting a pair of socks on her hands.

Carefully, she picked up the faded photo and waited for something bad to happen.

Nothing did, and she realized that the socks were an excellent barrier. "Not exactly a fashion statement, but it will work."

She perched on the edge of her bed, and examined the old image. Rhiannon knew she was looking at a very faded and grainy picture of Suzanne. Why had all of Suzanne's stuff been shoved in an old barn? Why didn't Jared's great-great grandpa keep her things with him when he moved?

Suzanne looked about seventeen, Rhiannon thought, and so stern and unsmiling in the picture. But she was still pretty, even in faded black and white. She was standing next to an older man, who Rhiannon recognized as Abediah Roberts from Suzanne's vision. Her father.

A shiver raced up her spine and she trembled. "Dang." The back of her neck prickled with goose bumps. "Suzanne?"

"*You made him angry. Stay away, Rhiannon.*"

"Me? Who are we talking about? Your father?" Rhiannon shook the picture, her hand all ridiculous-looking covered in a pink sock.

"*You don't understand. Stay away. Stay away! I was wrong to ask you to help me.*"

Suzanne's voice faded, and Rhiannon knew she hadn't imagined the fear in the spirit's tone. *Well, I am not giving into some one-hundred-year-old bully, and that is that. How much harm can a dead guy do?*

She thought of the black essence in the closet and at her fingertips, of her unnatural anger the day she'd faced Janet. "I'm thinking loads of damage. A one-spirit wrecking ball."

Rhee put the photo down, more determined than ever to find something with Suzanne's handwriting so that she could get it to Tanya.

There were plenty of letters, but they were all to Suzanne. She'd already seen the wedding invitation, and there were a few hair ties and a dried rose, but other than that, the box was empty.

Rhiannon noticed a slight bulge at the bottom of the hatbox. Curious, she picked at the cardboard with an envelope.

Don't get too excited, she thought, *it could be warped from old age, or maybe just sitting out in the shed for a hundred years, or...*

She impatiently pulled the socks off of her hands and yanked at the false bottom. Then she sucked in a stunned breath.

"Suzanne's diary!"

Chapter Seventeen

Rhiannon brought the diary over to the window, ready to curl up in her chair and finally get to Suzanne's secrets.

She glanced out for a quick sec, then bounced up from the chair, dropped the book, and squealed. "Jared! I totally forgot about my riding lesson. Of all the days..." She grabbed her boots and ran downstairs before he had a chance to come inside their house.

One look and he'd start asking questions. It was inevitable. Rhiannon's plan was to hide their family religion for as long as possible.

"Hey!" she yelled, a little out of breath from running down the stairs so fast. Then she tripped over her untied bootlace, landing in a humiliating sprawl on the grass.

Jared grinned down at her. "Excited about your riding lesson? Or just happy to see me?"

Rhiannon knew she had to be blushing all the way up to her hairline, which should blend in with her red roots. Even her ears were on fire.

She jumped to her feet, then knelt and tied the lace, hiding her face with her hair. When she thought it was safe to look at him without bursting into flames of never-to-be lived-down embarrassment, she said, "Ah, neither. I forgot you were coming over, and mom is baking and, oh... Never mind. Your horse is awesome."

She felt guilty, a little, because she knew that she wasn't going to tell Jared about Suzanne, even though the spirit was his ancestor. She couldn't tell anybody, not until she had the answers.

Jared dismounted, leading his horse over to the corral where Moonstone was watching them with interest. "I raised him from a foal. He's real fast, and a great jumper."

"Name?"

He kicked the grass with the toe of his cowboy boot. "Rocky."

Rhiannon giggled. "As in Sylvester Stallone? Or Rocky and Bullwinkle?"

Jared shot her an arrogant look. "Sylvester Stallone. *Rocky* is another classic movie. One of my favorites."

Rhiannon bit her lower lip so that she wouldn't keep laughing. "You did say you were a fan. I never got into those boxing movies, though. I prefer the flying squirrel."

Jared puffed out his chest. "You're such a girl," he teased.

Rhiannon flipped her hair. "Well, duh. I'm glad you noticed."

"I'm not blind."

Rhiannon couldn't think of anything funny to say to that so she walked away from him and over to Moonstone. "Hey, girl." Her stomach was a jumble of nerves. Why would Jared flirt with her? His twin hated her ever-loving guts, she was an official member of the Loser Club, and she was...different.

Was he just messing with her? Making her think that he liked her so that he could "dump" her in some completely humiliating and very public way?

Or maybe he thought that because she came from Vegas, she was easy.

Little did he know that she'd never even been kissed.

She asked over her shoulder, "Do we get to break out of the corral today? Please tell me I've graduated to beyond the circle."

He laughed. "Moonstone is an excellent horse. I think we can ride out through the woods, so long as you let me hold on to a lead."

Rhiannon lifted her eyes to the thick acreage of trees that lined their property, and separated her house from Jared's. "Won't we get lost?"

"Nah, there's a trail, there's even a small clearing. Perfect for picnics. Or if we go further in, we can see the lake."

Rhiannon shivered. She was staying clear of Crystal Lake until she figured out Suzanne's secrets. "The clearing sounds fine. Um, let me run in and tell my mom. Want a water bottle?"

"Sure. Do you want me to wait here?"

Rhiannon wondered if it was rude not to invite him in. It probably was, but it was better than having him see the altar dedicated to the Goddess that was in the middle of their living room.

"Uh, Mom's cleaning and stuff. I'll be back in a minute."

She left him with the horses and hurried. Her mom helped her fill a backpack with water, apples, and nut bread. "Thanks, Mom!" she said as she ran down the stairs, careful not to trip. Again.

"All set," she told Jared as she wiped a bead of sweat from her upper lip.

He gave her a strange look, but then shrugged. "Let's go!"

Once they were mounted and on their way, Rhiannon kept sneaking peeks at Jared. He looked incredible on his horse. He made riding seem so simple that even a dork could do it.

So why was she having such a hard time? She was grateful that Jared took his role as tour guide seriously. He sounded like a for-real documentary channel newscaster, pointing out everything from the trees to the bugs.

He didn't seem to need her to do anything more than nod or grunt occasionally, which was about all she could handle while hanging on for dear life.

"Don't run, Moonstone, not unless you want to kill me. It will be murder. You could do horsey jail time, I think."

The horse slapped her with her tail.

"Were you saying something?" Jared turned and asked.

Busted. She had to break the habit of talking out loud. "Uh, no. Moonstone and I are bonding."

"Great start." He gave her an approving smile. "A rider should always be friends with their horse." Jared paused and pointed through a thick stand of trees. He pushed through them and Rhiannon—well, Moonstone—followed. "Here's the clearing. What do you think?"

Rhiannon lightened her grip on the reins and looked around in awe. The sunlight fell through the leafy tree branches like light shining through stained glass windows.

"It's beautiful." A feeling of happiness washed over her and she tilted her chin up to the sun's rays.

Jared inched over to where she was sitting on Moonstone. Rhiannon's nerves went on high alert, but her horse stayed perfectly still. At least one of them kept their marbles around Jared.

"I had a feeling you'd like it."

Rhiannon rolled her eyes, trying to keep him at a distance. She was feeling a little shy. "'Cause I'm girly?" she teased.

Jared exhaled. "Nope."

"Why then?"

He smiled and her heart thumped. He said, "I dunno. Hungry?"

Rhiannon thought maybe she'd manage to choke down some water, but that was about all. She and Jared were one-hundred-percent alone. Just the two of them and their teenage hormones. In a romantic clearing in the woods. Moonstone side-stepped nervously, finally picking up on Rhiannon's tenseness.

"Uh, sure," she managed to say. What if he tried to kiss her? Would she kiss him back?

Or would she tell him she was a giant chicken baby who had never been kissed? A clueless fourteen-year-old who wasn't sure that kissing her enemy's twin brother was a great idea?

But man, he was so cute. And cool too.

She dismounted, not very gracefully, but it didn't matter since Jared wasn't looking; he was busy sweeping off the rocks before he sat down.

Rhee slowly walked over to where he was sitting. "Awesome! Did you put these here?"

He shook his head. "Huh-uh. They're great seats, though. My dad said that his dad made the fire pit, and he'd bring us here when we were kids, and roast marshmallows, make s'mores."

Rhiannon sat down and opened the pack. "Sounds like fun. I've never had a s'more."

Jared shoved his hat back on his head and stared at her in disbelief. "Rhiannon, that is plain wrong. Next time we come out here, I'll bring all the stuff. You'll see what you've been missin'."

Her heart skipped. He was already planning on bringing her back here, to this special spot. She handed him an apple and a slice of nut bread, one of her mom's specialties.

"Thanks."

"Thank you," Rhiannon answered awkwardly. "I mean, for Moonstone, and the riding lessons, and for bringing me here."

His eyes sparkled at her from beneath the brim of his hat, then he took a giant bite from the apple.

The awareness of one another was like a third person between them. Each time Jared's thigh brushed hers on the rock seat, Rhiannon practically jumped out of her skin.

She chewed slowly, wondering why she had to go and have a crush on someone as altogether great as Jared Roberts. What did he see in her?

Jared tossed the apple core into the trees.

"Isn't that littering?" Rhiannon asked as a way to break the tension.

"Nah, some squirrel will grab it."

Rhiannon stood and started gathering their supplies. "I guess we should go back."

Jared shrugged. "You sure you don't want to go on down to the lake?"

"Uh, yeah. I'm sure." No way could she admit to having a fear of a harmless body of water, just like she couldn't tell him why she had that irrational fear. It would so totally break the mood. She just stood there like an idiot, holding the backpack and nodding while he cocked his head to the right and studied her.

"Do I make you nervous?" He stepped forward, until the backpack was the only thing separating them.

Rhiannon gulped and lied. "Nope."

He smiled that lop-sided smile she thought was so cute. "Sure?"

Rhiannon wished that some mutant squirrel would come flying from the woods and whisk her away. It didn't happen.

She looked away. "I don't know. I keep wondering why you're flirting with me." There. Now he could tell her he wasn't flirting. He could tell her she was out of her mind and to stop imagining things.

"I like you."

She swiftly glanced up. "What?"

He took off his hat, and Rhiannon noticed he didn't even have hat hair. "I said that I like you."

Panic ran through her veins. This was not the scenario she'd had worked out in her head. Now what?

"Well?"

Rhiannon swallowed. "Well what?"

"Don't you like me?"

"All the girls like you."

Jared snorted. "Whatever. Can I kiss you?"

Rhiannon gripped the backpack. Her first kiss. *Oh, man.* Did she have apple in her teeth? She nodded, unable to speak, and pursed her lips, leaning forward.

Anticipation and the urge to feel Jared's lips on hers held her in a spell.

Which was broken by a snide voice saying, "Isn't this sweet?"

Rhiannon dropped the backpack to the ground, embarrassed and feeling like she'd been busted doing something wrong. Where on earth was that mutant, apple-core eating squirrel?

And why was Janet here?

Jared must have told her.

Rhee bent to gather the backpack, realizing she'd been had. She shook off Jared's hand from her arm, refusing to meet his gaze. He'd set her up on purpose. She knew it. *She was such an idiot! Why didn't she listen to her hunches?*

Humiliating tears burned her eyes and she blinked, blinked, blinked. She grit her teeth and bit the inside of her cheek.

"Hey, Jared." Janet's tone was frosty-cool. "Great day for a picnic."

"We already ate." Jared narrowed his eyes at his sister, but Rhiannon was too hurt to care. He was probably just trying to cover his tracks.

Why had she been so stupid? Why had she let down her guard? *Why, why, why?*

That icky feeling made loop-de-loops in her stomach, followed by a growing, uncontrollable anger. No. Not that, she warned her interior mad-o-meter.

Janet and her two best friends, Mutt and Jeff, as Rhiannon had nicknamed them, brought their horses farther into the clearing. Rhiannon quickly walked to Moonstone before she lost it completely.

Janet rode right by Moonstone, brushing her hand over the tip of the horse's ear. "Nice horse. Isn't that one of ours?" Janet asked Jared.

"It's Rhiannon's now."

"Ah, yes." Janet tapped her lower lip and grinned. "Spoiled little witch girl's parents picked her out just for you. And they paid for riding lessons. How much extra did they throw in for Jared to kiss you?"

"Janet!" Jared yelled.

Rhiannon now knew what it meant when someone said

they saw red. Red as in blood, red as in anger, red as in fury. Without meaning to, she envisioned Janet's horse rearing and Janet flying through the air to land on her butt in front of her friends and her brother. She imagined Janet all tied up in a body cast. Embarrassed, just like Rhee felt now.

And then Janet's horse stood up on its hind legs, catching her off guard. Rhiannon watched, already sorry, really sorry, as Janet tried to control her horse. Her friends called her name and tried to help. Jared ran dangerously close to the horse's flying hooves. Janet, her face pale and scared, happened to lock eyes with Rhiannon and it was as if Janet knew Rhiannon had wished it to happen.

And then Janet lost control and went falling to the ground, landing in a heap next to the rocks.

I'm going to be sick, Rhee thought.

Jared ran to the still form of his sister, and Rhiannon jumped up on Moonstone.

The apple she'd eaten was caught at the back of her throat, and she felt like she was going to hurl, adding even another pound of humiliation to her already heavy shoulders. How could she have wished something harmful like that? She hadn't meant to, but she couldn't exactly apologize!

Rhee swallowed and buried the guilt, remembering Janet's words. Janet had deserved it. She *had*! They all had.

That felt wrong too.

"I'll call for help!" Rhee said as she urged Moonstone toward home. None of them looked her way, but she didn't bother repeating herself. Hopefully, the horse would know how to get there, 'cause she sure didn't. But she had to leave, before she did anything worse.

She didn't understand why she couldn't control her temper.

How could she ever explain to Jared that she'd murdered his sister?

Chapter Eighteen

"My stomach really hurts."

Tucking the covers beneath Rhiannon's chin, her mom said, "All right, honey. You can stay home and sleep. I'll make some tea in a bit. Seeing your friend fall from her horse must have been horrible for you! You tossed and turned all night."

"Yeah. It sucked." Rhiannon hoped the guilt she felt wasn't written all over her face.

"Well, you know Janet is just fine. Mrs. Roberts said she would even be at school today."

Rhiannon closed her eyes, seeing Janet fly from her horse again and again. Her stomach gurgled as she remembered the thud Janet's body had made when it hit the ground. "I'm glad. Thanks for calling, Mom."

She turned on her side, facing the wall.

Her mom shut the door quietly behind her.

Rhee was safely snuggled up in the guest bedroom and she had absolutely no intentions of moving back into the attic. Ever. When she'd gotten home, she'd been covered with the black essence she'd come to associate with the evil in the closet.

She couldn't deal with stupid ghosts, or spirits—whatever they were—she was way out of her league. Rhee hated Crystal Lake and the Roberts family. She cringed at the thought of

159

facing Jared at school. How could he have been so mean? Pretending to like her, even pretending to want to kiss her. He was just as horrible as Janet.

Squeezing her eyes tightly closed didn't stop the hot trickle of tears down her cheeks. She'd been such a chump, believing that Jared had actually cared about her.

And it wasn't like she *meant* to make Janet's horse rear. Not really. Janet obviously needed to learn how to control her horse if she was going to ride one.

Rhiannon buried her head beneath the covers and wished she were back in Vegas, at the institute where Dr. Richards could keep her safe from ridicule. Tanya and Matthew could help her figure it out. She hadn't meant for Janet to fall from her horse, but then again, didn't Janet kind of have it coming? If Janet hadn't been mean, or insulting, or such a bully, then nothing bad would have happened. When she finally fell asleep she had convinced herself that it wasn't her fault.

By Tuesday, Rhiannon had a chip on her shoulder the size of Texas, certain that everybody hated her.

She bumped into Bonnie on the way to math class. "Hey," Rhiannon said coolly.

"Are you okay?" Bonnie asked as she struggled to keep up with Rhiannon's long strides.

Rhee noticed that Bonnie hadn't bothered to keep anything about her new look. She was dressed just as awful as usual. *Whatever.* She'd tried, but obviously Bonnie and Melody had just been pretending to like the makeover. "Fine," she answered in a clipped tone. "I had the flu."

"Oh. I tried to call you, but your mom said you were sleeping."

"Yeah, well, then I probably was." In reality, Rhiannon hadn't wanted to talk to anyone. She didn't know who to trust.

She was angry, and she knew it. She welcomed it. She didn't need these people; she was going to be a famous Doctor of Parapsychology.

Bonnie slowed her pace and said from behind her, "I heard about Janet's accident."

Rhiannon stopped in her tracks, waiting for Bonnie to tell her what an awful person she was. She turned and tapped her toe impatiently. This always happened when she left her comfort zone—eventually people found out what she could do, and they hated her. It was better to just be done with trying.

Scrunching up her nose, Bonnie said, "It's just too weird. I mean, Janet is an excellent rider. She's always winning ribbons and stuff at the state fairs. I can't believe she lost control of her horse."

Rhiannon shuffled her feet. "Looks like Janet's not as perfect as everybody thought."

Bonnie's eyes widened and Rhee turned to walk into the math room by herself. So what if she'd hurt her feelings. Bonnie probably never liked her anyway.

She sauntered into class, prepared to give Jared the cold shoulder.

He saw her and sneered.

She blinked in surprise. He was mad at *her*? How dare he give her a dirty look when he was the one who had set her up in the first place!

If he hadn't embarrassed her *on purpose*, she never would have accidentally sent Janet's horse rearing. The Roberts had gotten what they deserved for playing such a mean trick on her.

She flipped her hair and stalked by his seat. He leaned across the row and whispered to his friends, who looked back at her and glared.

She pretended she didn't care.

By lunch, nobody was speaking to her. Well, the kids at the Loser table, but even they were unusually quiet. Her nerves felt stretched to the breaking point. Bonnie kept giving her hurt looks, Melody wouldn't say anything at all, and Broomstick stared down at the table like he was afraid of her.

Rhiannon finally tossed down her cheese sandwich. "What?"

Corey, for once, wasn't in a teasing mood. "Janet and her friends are saying that you deliberately made her horse rear. I know you wanted revenge, but Janet could have been killed."

Rhiannon's cheeks burned as she defended herself. "And just how did I manage to do that?" *I should tell them how right they are.*

He waved with his hot dog, spreading ketchup on the table like blood. "They're saying that you did it so that Jared wouldn't ride with Janet at the rodeo. That you wanted to ride with Jared, and be crowned the rodeo princess."

Rhiannon broke out into hurt laughter. "I don't wanna be a stupid princess!"

"I'm just telling you what the rumors are. Janet's saying that you put something underneath her saddle, to irritate her horse."

Rhiannon's mouth dropped open. "But, I... That is the most ridiculous thing I've ever heard." Even though she was *sort of* responsible for making Janet fall, the story that Corey was repeating to her was not true. "I was nowhere near her horse's saddle."

Janet had been knocked out for a second, stunned, but fine. One of Janet's friends, either Mutt or Jeff, had ridden back to the Roberts' house, and gotten there way before Rhee had even made it home. Jared's mom had told Starla that when they'd reached the clearing Janet was already back on her horse.

Janet was just making trouble.

Rhee fumed.

Corey said, "Janet's reminding everyone that you threatened to get even with her for the milk on your shoes thing. The whole lunchroom heard you tell her she would regret what she did."

Broomstick pointed a skinny finger at her, "We saw the posters."

Rhiannon felt like a giant axe was waiting to fall across her neck. She hated school. *Hated it, hated it.* Just like everybody hated her. "What posters?"

Bonnie reached into her backpack and pulled out a wadded-up piece of construction paper. "Here. I didn't want to believe it, so I tore it down. I was gonna ask you about it, later, when you were in a better mood."

Rhiannon sat up straight and set her mouth in a thin line. Her fingers were shaking as she unfolded the paper. She read it once. She read it twice. Her eyes filled with tears and the words blurred on the page. *This is so unfair!*

Corey patted her awkwardly on the back, and Bonnie handed her a napkin.

Melody said slowly, "I guess you didn't make that poster?"

Rhiannon shook her head, unable to speak. Then she took a breath and told them what had really happened, that Janet and her friends had come to the clearing. That Jared was giving Rhiannon riding lessons. That Janet just lost control of her horse. "I don't know why," she finished the truth with a lie.

Melody sighed. "Then this is Janet's revenge. You saw her fall, which would be very embarrassing for her."

Everybody at the table nodded. "Janet's a great rider," Broomstick said sadly. "And we all know that Janet will do anything to *not* be a loser."

Meat took the crumpled paper and read aloud, "Rhiannon Godfrey challenges Janet Roberts at the Bronco Riding competition. Newcomer from Las Vegas, Nevada to take title from reigning Crystal Lake Champ."

"What title?" Rhiannon wiped her eyes. Her voice was shaky as she said, "Listen. I just learned how to saddle my own horse. I can't jump. I can't go faster than a slow trot. What the heck is a *bronco* competition?"

Corey groaned. "Bucking Bronco? Where you're strapped to a mean horse that's doing its very best to scrape you off on the fence so he can trample you until you're nothing but a pile of broken bones. You've never heard of that?"

Broomstick said, "It's *the* event of the rodeo! They have clowns who jump out of barrels to serve as a distraction so that the rider doesn't get killed when he or she falls off."

Rhiannon pressed her knuckles to her mouth. "I can't do that!"

Meat finished his Vienna sausage. "You have to. Unless you want to move to another town and change your name. You can't back out of a challenge."

"But I didn't make those posters—"

Broomstick shook his head. "Doesn't matter. Too many people have heard what happened between you and Janet. These are all over school—you can't back down."

"Unless you break your leg or something," Bonnie added helpfully.

Rhee shuddered. She was trapped. How on earth was she going to get out of this scrape?

It was all Janet's fault!

The Losers rallied around her, coming up with a few more helpful solutions on ways to injure herself. Rhiannon soaked up their good intentions, realizing that she'd almost dumped her friends without giving them a chance. She'd been scared to lose them, so she pushed them away.

Talk about not logical. What was happening to her science-minded brain?

Melody grabbed the poster and balled it back up. "I sure hope you have medical insurance."

"I appreciate the help, guys, really, but I need to come up with something else."

The bell rang, and school was finally over. Head down, Rhiannon walked straight for the double doors leading outside.

"Hey!"

Rhiannon heard Jared calling to her, but she kept walking. The last thing she needed was another confrontation where she ended up feeling like crap.

"Rhiannon, wait."

Feeling the drop of his hand on her shoulder, she stopped, bracing herself against his anger.

"Why did you do it?"

"Which part?" She lifted her chin with false bravado. No way was she going to let Jared know how much he'd hurt her.

He pointed to a brightly colored *Rhiannon versus Janet* poster on the wall.

She shrugged him off. "I didn't make those."

He snorted. "Yeah, right. I don't know how you did it, but you could have killed my sister with your stupid prank. She is gonna kick your butt in that competition. You don't even know how to ride a regular horse. What makes you think you can ride a bronc? You could really get hurt."

Rhiannon tried not to flinch as he skewered her with his eyes. Why did he care about whether or not she broke her neck? He'd set her up in the first place!

"Don't worry about me," she said with a fake smile.

"Why are you being this way?" Jared brushed his hair back from his forehead, annoyance on his face. "Being popular is so important that you're willing to risk people's lives? That's just stupid, I thought you were cooler than that."

Ouch. The accusation hurt and she opened her mouth to explain that he had it all wrong, she didn't want to be popular, she wanted to be accepted, but then she stopped. Jared had been playing her all along.

Hadn't he?

He looked genuinely mad. She probed, just a tiny mind tickle, and realized that he was a little hurt too. *By her?*

Rhiannon quickly re-evaluated her reasons for thinking Jared had deliberately set her up as a joke. His twin sister had hated her at first sight.

She'd wondered if he'd always had a separate agenda, but until the scene at the clearing he'd seemed as terrific as Janet was terrible.

Rhee frowned, remembering the look in his eyes as he'd flirted with her, and when he'd leaned down to kiss her—yes, she'd been embarrassed, but not by Jared—*by Janet.* If Jared had really wanted to help Janet out and humiliate Rhiannon, he would have set her up in a more public spot.

Goddess help her, what if she'd made a monumental error in judgment?

Again?

She'd already misjudged her friends. Rhiannon wasn't feeling too good about herself so she spoke quickly, "I didn't stick anything under her saddle. I wouldn't hurt an animal, and besides, you know I was nowhere near Janet. You were right there, Jared."

He stepped back from her, his lip curled up. "Don't remind me. I wish I never had taken you to the clearing. You just stay away from there, got it? And as for the rest of your riding lessons? Well, I quit. You'd be smart to back out of that competition."

Rhiannon's chin trembled but she didn't dare cry. Jared was furious with her and she had a sinking feeling that she might have jumped to the wrong conclusion in the clearing. Jared didn't look like he'd be into forgiving her any time soon. She jerked her shoulders back like she didn't care, but her anger had to go somewhere and the strap on her backpack snapped in two, spilling her books and papers to the floor.

Sighing, she knelt down. This was *so* her rotten life.

"Ooh, what's this?"

Rhiannon's jaw clenched. Whenever anything bad happened, Janet just had to be there to gloat. She ignored her and tried to gather the papers as fast as possible.

She wasn't fast enough. Janet bent down and slid a piece of notebook paper from underneath her math book. She dangled the paper like a prize between her fingers.

"Geez, Jared. It looks like Brianna has a real crush on you. She's written your name all over, with little hearts around it. Kiss, kiss."

Janet's laughter was mean, but didn't hurt near as bad as Jared's short bark of disbelief.

It was like salt on an open wound when he added, "I wouldn't let my dog kiss her."

The kids in the hall laughed while Rhiannon hung her head and tried to keep her cool. This was her worst nightmare, and it sucked as bad as she'd feared.

It was Janet's own fault that she couldn't stay on her horse when it reared. She's just mad because she's supposed to be some riding diva, and I saw her fall on her rear.

I thought that Jared had set me up, but now I don't know. He's too mad at me to be guilty of trying to embarrass me on purpose.

Which means that he might have really liked me. Talk about something being so over.

She hated Janet Roberts.

Well, Rhiannon wasn't going to just let her win. No way, that wasn't her style. *I'll figure out how to ride a bronco, even if I have to use my psychic powers to kick butt!* One thing for sure, Janet was going down.

She blinked back furious tears as Janet ripped the incriminating note to shreds. Within a millisecond the torn pieces of paper were raining down over her head like confetti.

Somehow she didn't think the pain and humiliation she was feeling could be described as part of a normal high school experience.

Chapter Nineteen

"My dad rented a mechanical bull," Rhiannon told Tanya. Seated on the couch with her legs curled beneath her, she had the phone in one hand and a secret bite-sized candy bar in the other. She quickly tucked the phone between her ear and shoulder, unwrapping the chocolate and popping into her mouth. Her mom tried to tell her that an apple was just as good. *Right.*

"No way, that is so cool!"

Rhee swallowed. "Not really. I'm one big giant bruise from falling, but they totally bought my story about wanting to ride the bronco in the rodeo. Mom was freaked at first, but she checked into the rules and stuff. We have to wear helmets and protective gear."

"I wish I could be there, but my mom just signed me up for a new series of lectures on telekinesis. Like there's a cure for it or something."

"You won't miss much, just me looking like an idiot. I'll probably last about two seconds, and Janet will be able to laugh her head off as she accepts her blue stinking ribbon and they haul me away in an ambulance."

Tanya laughed. "I think it's awesome that your parents let you try new stuff. They completely support you."

Rhiannon sighed. "They took me away from the institute. How is that supporting me?"

"They wanted you to have a regular high school experience."

"And getting my body hurled from an angry bronco is normal?"

"Wuss."

"Ha."

"How's Suzanne?"

"Don't know. I, uh, moved out of the attic. I took over the extra bedroom on the second floor. Things got a little creepy." Rhiannon felt a twinge of guilt for not telling Tanya about what had *really* happened with Janet in the clearing. She was terrified that somehow she was becoming the black essence, and if she wasn't careful, maybe she'd turn all black and rotten inside. Even worse than Janet, and that was seriously messed up.

She just didn't want to think about it at all.

"I think it's time to call Dr. Richards."

And admit to another failure? No thanks. "Right now I'm concentrating on surviving my first rodeo. Then I might take on Suzanne's problems again. How are things there?"

"All right. Boring, actually. It's the same old routine. School in the morning, classes in the afternoon. I'm actually looking forward to being in Utah next month."

"Doing what?"

"A small group of mainstream scientists want to test my psychic abilities, and publish their findings in Science Week. Doc will get a byline."

"That's very cool. If anybody can convince stodgy non-believers that parapsychology is a real science, it will be you."

"I dunno. I always liked it better when we went as a team. The telepathic twosome. I miss you, Rhee."

"I miss you too...in fact, you should be here. I'm having some friends over for a slumber party."

Tanya sighed, loud and deep. "Lucky. Remember hanging out in the game room here? You, me and the Mattster."

"I remember you getting your butt whipped in ping pong!"

Giggling, Tanya said, "Matthew's just not the same lately."

Rhiannon chewed her bottom lip. "He's just pushing your buttons. He told me once that he likes how your eyes get all crazy when he makes you mad."

"Ah!"

"Hey, I talked Mom into buying soda *and* chips. She even put away her Goddess altar."

"You haven't told your friends that your family is Wiccan?"

"Nah. I'm hoping to pass every weird thing off as New Age. The whole subject of witchcraft can be a little freaky for people."

"Freaky? Not once you explain that you aren't into a bunch of hocus pocus. Even my mom got that, and she has to be the most judgmental person who ever took a breath."

"Your mom is from the *city*. She's seen the world. These people think Wal-Mart is a big deal." A knock sounded on the front door. "I gotta go. I'll call you tomorrow, okay?"

She hung up, then answered the door. Melody and Bonnie were on the porch, loaded down with sleeping bags and suitcases.

"You said to bring clothes." Melody laughed, then turned to wave at the pick up truck idling in the driveway. After a single honk, the driver waved back and left.

"Your mom?"

"Yeah. She's late for work."

Rhiannon opened the door wide, "Come on in."

"Wow!" Bonnie said. "Awesome house. We've driven by here a million times, and I had no clue it was this huge inside."

Melody dropped her stuff by the stairs. "This is great. I love the fireplace. Where are we sleeping?"

"I thought down here, so that we could hang out in front of the fire."

Bonnie said, "Ooh, and tell ghost stories."

Rhiannon tried to smile. "If you want." She could tell them a doozie.

Her mom came in from the laundry room. "Merry meet—"

"Mom!" Rhiannon cut in. "This is Melody, and Bonnie."

"Welcome," her mom shot her a look, but then sighed. "Didn't your mom come in, Melody? I was hoping to meet her. She sounded so nice over the telephone."

"She said to tell you she's sorry, but she got called in early for work. Next time she'll come in."

"Oh. What does she do?"

"She's a waitress." Rhiannon heard something off in her friend's voice, and wondered what Melody's mom must be like.

"That is a tough job, I admire anyone who can do that." Starla shook her head and said, "Remind me to send you home with some sea salt and rosehip for a foot soak. Would you girls like something to drink?"

Her friends smiled and nodded and exchanged a glance as Starla hustled away. "Wow," they said at the same time.

Melody added, "Your mom is so cool. And pretty too. You look like her."

Rhiannon shrugged. She didn't want to be like her mom.

"We have the same color eyes and hair, that's all."

"I would love to have a mom who cared about being pretty. Mine still isn't talking to me about my makeover. It's like it never happened."

"I would like to have a mom who was around, period," Melody said.

"Does she work a lot?"

Bonnie shook her head behind Melody's back and Rhiannon wished she'd kept her curiosity to herself.

Melody ignored her anyway, and walked around the living room. "I can't believe all the candles you have. They smell great! And crystals hanging in the corners..."

She halted suddenly and turned to stare at Rhiannon. Starla entered with a tray of drinks and sliced fruit. "Here we are, girls."

Rhiannon bit her lip as she watched Melody *really* notice the Celtic amulet around her mom's neck and the multitude of jingly bracelets up and down her arms.

Bonnie sat on the couch and accepted a glass. "Thank you, Mrs. Godfrey."

"You're welcome. And call me Starla. Mrs. Godfrey sounds so old," her mom said with a shiver.

Melody said, "Starla is a beautiful name."

Her mom smiled. "I do like it. I was named for—"

"Mom!"

Her mom blinked. "Right. I'll just be in the kitchen if you need anything."

Rhiannon sank into the couch. Her mom was so *embarrassing*.

Starla stuck her head around the corner. "I caught that,

Rhiannon!"

"Sorry."

Melody snickered. "I think you have some explaining to do."

Rhiannon blushed and launched into yet another fabrication. She hoped she could keep all her whoppers in order. "Well, my mom is really into the New Age stuff. Health food and beads and all that. She and my dad are making our barn into a New Age shop, Celestial Beginnings."

"Now, that is awesome. And you're sitting there like you want to disappear when you have it so cool."

Bonnie sipped her drink. "My mom is very religious. We have church on Sunday and Wednesday. No excuses."

"I hate church," Melody said. "So, can we see your room?"

Rhiannon froze on the couch. What were the chances that Suzanne would stay hidden? And behave? "Um, okay."

So long as it was daylight and they kept the door open *and* she had her shields up before entering the room, maybe it would be all right.

Melody arched her brow in question. "Rhee?"

"Yeah." Rhiannon pointed to the stairs. "Go all the way up."

Bonnie said, "I can't wait to see the skylight you were talking about."

Rhiannon prepared for the worst as she followed her friends into her room.

Nothing. They were alone.

Melody and Bonnie hopped on the bed and lay back against the pillows. Bonnie giggled. "This is the best room I've ever seen!"

"Yeah," Melody agreed. "This is magazine cool. You are so lucky."

Rhiannon felt pretty lucky. Lucky that her resident ghosts were staying out of sight. Maybe they were afraid of strangers.

Melody bounded off the bed and started looking at all the shelves of books and knick-knacks. Then she found the closet. Rhee was glad that she'd remembered to remove the padlock before her friends had come over.

Melody opened the door and flipped on the light.

Rhiannon tensed, then exhaled with relief when nothing happened. For example, no black stuff exploded everywhere.

Squealing, Melody said, "I knew it! This is practically a mall. Not a single ugly piece of clothing. You have great taste, Rhee. And you're my size."

It was dark before Rhiannon realized where the time had gone. She felt a cold breeze from the open closet and then a *thunk* when something fell off of her shelf.

Melody, who looked awesome in a black blazer and a crimson velvet miniskirt, turned and looked at the floor. "What was that?"

Leaning over, she picked it up and read the cover. "Ha! This, Bonnie, is Rhiannon's diary."

Rhiannon jumped to her feet and tried to grab the book from Melody's fingers. "Give that back."

"Nope. You have secrets, Rhiannon, and inquiring minds want to know."

Bonnie must have noticed Rhiannon's panic. "Let her have it back, Melody. You wouldn't want anybody reading your diary, would you?"

Melody paused and then read the title. "Rhiannon's grim...grimoire? What does that mean?"

A slight wind that nobody else seemed to notice besides her ruffled the curtains, and Rhee winced.

"Book of secrets?" Melody kept reading, quickly turned a few of the pages and then faced Rhiannon. Her look was accusing. "This is a book of spells."

Bonnie gasped and dropped the shirt she'd been admiring as if it had burned her fingers.

"Suzanne," Rhiannon muttered under her breath. *Why did you do that?* Was this payback for moving out of the attic for a few days?

Oh, pay back, Rhiannon thought angrily. *Just you wait, Suzanne.*

Melody shut the book with a snap. "Your family isn't New Age. Janet was totally right about you from the beginning! You guys are witches."

"It's not like that," Rhiannon said as her friends stared at her like she'd developed green skin and a long nose with a wart.

Melody tapped her foot. "Spit it out, Rhee. Do you do these spells?"

Bonnie stayed on the bed as if she'd been turned to stone.

Rhiannon wanted to cry. *So much for having friends.* They'd be calling their parents as soon as they could to come and take them home—unless she could make them understand!

"Um. Well. Have you ever heard of Wicca?"

Melody nodded, listening but skeptical. Bonnie's face was pale. Rhiannon tried to find a way to explain without freaking them out.

"Wicca is a real religion. We pray to the Goddess."

Bonnie asked quietly, "Do you make sacrifices?"

"Not like that!" Rhiannon was on the verge of tears. "It is very similar to other religions. We believe in good, but unlike some of the Christian religions, we don't believe in Satan, and well, we believe in magick. Or at least, my parents do. I'm not sure what I believe."

Melody sank into the recliner next to the window. "I can't believe you keep this a secret. How come?"

Bonnie yelled, "I wish you would have kept your dumb secret forever! How can you believe in that stuff? It's wrong!"

Rhiannon straightened her shoulders. "Everybody has the right to choose a belief system."

Melody jumped up from the chair and plopped down on the bed next to Bonnie. She put her arm around her friend. "It's okay, Bon. It's not like she can cast spells to hurt people, right?"

Rhiannon's tongue was stuck to the roof of her mouth. She swallowed. "You aren't supposed to. What you send out comes back to you three-fold. If you send out evil, you will receive evil."

Bonnie's cheeks reddened. "So your mom is a witch? Your dad too?"

"Bonnie! My mom does kitchen magick, like herbs and stuff. It isn't like *Bewitched*. Nobody snaps their fingers and disappears. It's more like common sense, earth magick. How to use nature's bounty in order to heal."

Melody nodded. "That's the kind of stuff my grandma does. But she doesn't call it magick."

Rhiannon shrugged. "My parents might be eccentric, but they wouldn't harm a fly." She took the grimoire from Melody. "This book is something that we're taught to use in order to write down certain spells or chants that we like. It is personal for everyone. I mean, the first spell I wrote was so silly. I made a rhyme so that I would wake up with a piece of candy underneath my pillow."

Bonnie sniffed. "Did it work?"

Rhiannon smiled sadly. "Yeah." She held up a hand before

Bonnie's eyes popped out of her head. "My dad put it there during the night. That's when I started to realize that maybe magick wasn't real."

Melody's answering smile was understanding. "Man, it sucks when you find out that there is no such thing as Santa Claus."

Bonnie slowly let go of the shirt she'd been strangling. "When I first met you, Rhiannon, I thought that I had never met such a lonely person. Wasn't I right about that? But I like being your friend. I just don't know about *this*."

Rhiannon dipped her head. "I'm so glad that you're my friends. And we don't have to talk about religion. In fact—" she knew her smile was pleading, "—I would prefer it. Like, especially if you didn't tell anyone, ever?"

Melody sighed. "All right. We'll keep your secret."

Bonnie frowned, but then put out her hand, palm down. Melody smacked hers over Bonnie's and Rhiannon placed hers on top of theirs. "To friends!"

Then Rhiannon hustled them downstairs before Suzanne did something else and revealed another secret that Rhiannon wanted to keep to herself.

Letting them know she was Wiccan was the easy part.

What would they do if they knew she saw ghosts and could move things with her mind?

Chapter Twenty

The barn was warm, and the windows were steamy from all the hot air inside. Rhiannon said, "Put it up to five!"

Melody shook her head. "That's kinda fast, Rhee. Are you sure?"

Rhiannon wasn't sure at all, but she didn't want to lose to Janet, either. There was only one week left until the rodeo, and she was discovering a pretty thick competitive streak. "Yup."

The mechanical bull picked up speed. She held on to the handle of the saddle for all she was worth and gritted her teeth.

She thought of Janet's smug face every time they passed in the hall. She pictured Jared, who glared and went out of his way to avoid her.

Rhiannon wished he would talk to her. Since realizing that maybe she had overreacted in the clearing, she wanted to make peace with Jared. But he was having none of it.

He'd become a staunch supporter in his sister's campaign for freshman princess at the October rodeo.

Well, Rhiannon didn't care about some stupid crown. All she cared about was not breaking her neck.

Her concentration slipped and she fell from the saddle to the mat with a jolt that probably chipped a back tooth.

"You okay?" Bonnie peered over at her.

Rhiannon did a mental inventory. "Yeah. Nothing broken."

"That's the best time at that speed yet," Melody said proudly. "You might not die after all."

"Geez, thanks."

"No prob. Okay, I have to get home. Chores."

Rhiannon knew that Melody stayed as late as she could, but since she walked home alone, her mom was rigid about it being before dark. And her stubborn friend refused to accept a ride from anybody else's parent.

"Yeah, me too," Bonnie said.

Rhee knew that Bonnie left at the same time so that she could walk as far as possible with Melody. Her friends were cool. No matter what Janet said. "See you tomorrow, guys."

She waved goodbye to her friends and walked into the house. Her mom was busy making dinner and Rhiannon grabbed a water bottle and sat at the counter.

She tore the label off the bottle, wishing she had the guts to call Jared.

"So, why don't you?"

Rhiannon raised her eyes. "Mom!"

Starla smiled and finished peeling a potato. "Well, you're sitting right there. Sulking. Why don't you call him? He seems like such a sweet boy."

Hah, Rhiannon thought. *That sweet boy wants to hang me from the nearest tree.*

A confused look passed over her mom's face. "That *can't* be right."

Rhiannon laughed. "I'm gonna take Moonstone out for a ride before dinner, okay?"

"Be back in half an hour."

Moonstone's stall was next to Betsy's and Rhiannon would swear that the two of them were best friends. She fed Betsy a red petunia and patted her velvet nose.

"Come on, Moonstone. How about a short ride? Betsy, we'll be back before you're finished regurgitating your snack."

The cow mooed and swished her tail.

The horse whinnied and pranced from her stall.

Rhiannon decided without conscious thought to follow the path to the clearing. It would be the first time she tried to find the place on her own and she hoped she didn't get lost.

"Take me to the clearing, Moonstone. I'm following your lead, girl."

She was filled with a feeling of apprehension as they came closer to their destination. She had been so good about keeping her anger under control for the past few weeks. But she'd also stayed clear of the evil spirit in her closet. She'd come to a few conclusions about that stuff. She figured that the thing inside was somehow poisoning her, so she kept away. Her parents said that they wanted to install a different carpet in her room, making it easy to stay in the spare bedroom instead.

Which meant staying away from Suzanne too. How *had* Suzanne died? As soon as the rodeo was over, then, Rhiannon promised under her breath, she would read Suzanne's diary and try and solve the puzzle.

And if things got dangerous, she would call in Dr. Richards and Mrs. Edwards. She wasn't a *complete* moron.

Rhiannon took a deep breath of crisp air. It was October, and she had survived over a month of school. The leaves were turning colors on the trees, she had made some good friends, and she was actually looking forward to riding a bronco.

She laughed out loud and the sound echoed around her.

Moonstone neighed and Rhiannon's heart skipped when a horse neighed back.

She went through the trees, worried that she might be intruding on Janet and her friends.

She blinked. Jared sat in front of a small fire, poking it with a stick.

I should leave.

"What are you doing? I thought I said not to come here."

"This is the first time." She jerked her chin in the air at his attitude. What had she ever seen in him? "I'm going."

"You'd better."

Hurt feelings washed over her like stinging sleet and she guided Moonstone around in the direction toward home.

Jared said, "Wait."

She stopped, her head held high.

"Why did you run away?"

Confused, she turned all the way around again. "What?"

He stood and dropped the stick into the flames. "Why did you run away the day Janet got hurt?"

"I didn't! I rode all the way home as fast as I could to go and get help."

"You never called."

"My mom called your mom the minute she understood what I was saying. I was so scared, I probably wasn't making much sense. And your mom said that either Mutt or Jeff, I forget which one, had already been to your place and that Janet was okay."

His lips curved in that lop-sided smile and her pulse sped. "Mutt or Jeff?"

Rhiannon blushed. "I'm sorry. Your sister's friends. I can't tell them apart."

"They never told me that you had called. I thought that you ran away so that you wouldn't get in trouble. Not that you would have, so I didn't understand. Not unless you'd done something wrong. And then Janet said you put something under her horse's saddle. I checked, though, and never found anything. Plus, you did tell her you were going to pay her back, in front of the whole school."

Rhiannon slipped off of Moonstone's back, deciding to set things as right as she could. "I thought you set me up."

"What?" It was his turn to be confused, and Rhiannon enjoyed the moment.

It was time to clear the air between them. She might not get his friendship back, but at least she could be honest about this one thing.

"I didn't think you could ever like someone like me. So I thought you had your sister and her friends come to the clearing on purpose, so that I'd be embarrassed—well, make that humiliated—when I told you how much I liked you, and then you could totally mock me, and tell me how much you despised me in front of witnesses. I know Janet hates my guts. I know that she would really hate it if we, you know—" Rhiannon prodded the ground with her sneaker, "—were to go out, or anything. And so then I figured that you were just doing your sister a favor, and making sure I knew I'd never fit in at Crystal Lake."

Jared was silent. He looked at her without blinking for a full minute. Rhee counted the seconds, since she was holding her breath.

"That is the stupidest thing I have ever heard in my life."

Color flooded her face and she stared at the tips of his shoes. "I know."

"Really stupid."

"I know."

"That's like something from an MTV reality show. They'll do anything for ratings."

Rhee couldn't stop a small smile. "My previous life was more ratings oriented."

They stood in silence for a few more seconds before Jared spoke. "It took a lot of guts for you to tell me, you know, how you felt."

She nodded, her stomach curled as tight as a fist.

"Because then I could tell my sister, and she'd tell the school."

"That's true. But after what's already happened, it doesn't matter as much as *me* telling *you* that I'm sorry. You just aren't the kind of person who sets people up, and I should have trusted my instincts. I'm always second-guessing myself. And, well, I've never had a boyfriend, not that you were my boyfriend, a guy—there are lots of things I've never—" Rhiannon quit babbling and glanced at him from the corner of her eye.

He was grinning and shaking his head. "I've been here practically every day, hoping that you'd show up."

She tilted her head to the side, feeling some of the hot blush leave her skin. "But you told me not to come."

"At the time I said that, I thought that you were an immature brat who had an unreasonable vendetta against my sister. But I liked you anyway."

"You embarrassed me in front of everybody," she pointed out, remembering Janet, the confetti in the hallway and Jared's humiliating words.

"I didn't mean it."

"You could have said something at school!"

"Nope." He lowered his voice. "After telling everyone what a baby you were, I couldn't exactly talk to you, now could I?"

Rhiannon put her hand on her hip. "I am so *not* a baby."

Jared laughed and lifted a strand of her red hair, which flashed with gold in the setting sun. "Just a babe. You know you actually have some of Janet's friends betting money on you to win at the rodeo?"

Rhiannon's eyes flew open. "What?"

"Yup. Your friends have been letting it out that you're practicing on a mechanical bull. That's swaying the vote a little."

Rhiannon's knees wobbled. "Um, listen. I'm just trying not to break my neck."

"If my sister doesn't get princess, she'll do it for you."

Rhiannon looked into Jared's face. He was laughing. With her, instead of at her.

"Want to sit down? I've got graham crackers, marshmallows, and chocolate."

"Seriously?" Rhiannon sat down on the rock that was just big enough for two. She was incredibly, cautiously, happy.

"Yeah. Like I said, I was hoping you'd show up. So that I could tell you that I'm sorry."

She fought the suicidal urge to blurt every secret she'd ever had.

Had he meant what he said? Had he really been waiting here for her?

Jared leaned toward her just as she looked up from the flames. Her face was warm, her mouth parted to say she was sorry too.

His lips landed on hers and she found that she couldn't say anything at all as she was swept away by the magick of her very first kiss.

Chapter Twenty-One

Rhiannon shut her locker door with a slam, accidentally catching the sleeve of her sweater in the metal. She yanked, and it ripped. "Dang it!"

"Need some help?"

Rhiannon sighed. If it wasn't Janet witnessing her humiliation, then it would have to be Jared. Jared, who had kissed her yesterday in the clearing. Jared, who she had dressed to impress today. Well, she thought, that didn't exactly work out how I planned. *So much for cool and collected.*

She yanked harder and the sweater pulled free, trailing little yarn ends down her arm. "No. I got it. Thanks."

Rhee leaned forward to bang her head on the locker.

Jared huffed and pulled her back. "You're so funny. I wanted to...uh...ask if you wanted me to still give you riding lessons? Or maybe you could give me lessons."

"Huh?" Lessons with what?

"On the mechanical bull."

"Ooh. You want to come over and play." Her stomach flipped. She was actually flirting! She wouldn't even think about the fact that he could be using her to see how much of a chance she had against Janet.

He laughed and she could see that he really did like her too. *As much as she liked him?* Wow, she hoped so.

She pushed her hair away from her face and smiled. "Okay. You can come over after school, but no giving away my secrets."

He pretended to zip his lips. Then he changed his mind and kissed her, right there in front of everybody. "See ya later, Rhiannon."

Oh, yeah. Her stomach was a gaggle of butterflies. Or was that a swarm of butterflies? Who cared?

She turned and ran into Janet.

Figured.

"Nice sweater, Brianna."

Rhee raised a brow, but didn't say anything.

"Was that Jared I saw?"

Rhiannon felt the smile slip from her face and her fists clenched. Janet's wicked eyes narrowed and Rhee said belligerently, "So?"

Janet's green eyes were slits and she leaned in close. "I wasn't going to say anything, but since you look so...gullible, I guess I'd better."

Rhiannon so did not want to hear whatever Janet had to say. Janet's two friends giggled.

"I'm not interested," Rhee said and turned away.

Janet grabbed her arm. "Oh, but you should be. My older brother Brian bet Jared that he couldn't hook up with you by the rodeo. I tried to tell Bri you'd be easy, but he didn't believe me. He put ten bucks on the table."

Rhiannon's legs shook and she sucked in a shocked breath. She knew her eyes were so big they probably looked like blue ping-pong balls.

Oh, man, that hurt. It hurt really bad. She blinked and wished that Janet would just go away and leave her alone. Had the kiss she and Jared shared meant something different than what she'd thought?

No. She wouldn't make the same mistake of blaming Jared without talking to him first. "I don't believe you. You're just trying to cause trouble, as usual. The fact that your brother likes me must make you insane. He picked me over you."

Janet stepped forward, pointing at Rhiannon. "If you think you can break up our family, forget it. We Roberts stick together. Jared will see what kind of freak you are. Celestial Beginnings? Please," Janet snorted. "Witches R Us, more like it."

Rhiannon's heart thundered behind her ribcage, but she kept quiet.

"Cat got your tongue, Brianna? Or are you thinking of a spell to win my brother's heart?" Janet glanced at her friends, who laughed on cue. "You'll need something if you think he'll ever date you. Loser."

"If I was going to do a spell on anybody, it'd be you." She glared, knowing she should keep her mouth shut. Janet was as toxic as arsenic, and Rhee's temper boiled hot. The tips of her ears started to tingle, and she knew that if she stayed, she'd pile the lockers on Janet's body until the girl was squished.

Janet whistled. "Is that a threat?"

"A promise." The taste of putrid lake water rose in her throat and she choked. In that instant it became crystal clear that no matter how much she liked Jared they could never date. She and Janet couldn't get along, which meant that she'd always worry that Jared would take Janet's side over hers, like he'd done before. She stared into Janet's vicious green eyes, and her knees jerked as she saw how much Jared's twin despised her, and Goddess help her, she hated Janet right back.

The black essence in the closet was tied into what happened at Crystal Lake, with Suzanne—and it was evil; Rhiannon knew that as surely as she knew her own name.

When she was around Janet, Rhee felt like she was in danger of becoming a part of that blackness, and it terrified her. Her options sucked. Lose control and get vacuumed into a mystical darkness where it was possible that she'd have to haunt the farmhouse for eternity—or break up with Jared, and maybe live to see tenth grade.

She turned and ran.

"Chicken." Janet laughed after her.

Rhiannon ran through the halls, past Corey and Meat. She ran to Jared's classroom, and saw him sitting at his desk. *This wasn't his fault.* She walked down the row, concentrating on putting one step in front of the other, knowing that even though it broke her heart, she was doing the right thing.

The best thing.

So why was she so freaking angry?

She stopped in front of him, his crooked smile turning her insides to jelly. Chaotic emotions, when would she be able to control them?

"Hey, Rhee."

Maintaining eye contact so that she didn't accidentally flip over a desk or do some other dumb thing, she said, "I know about your brother's stupid bet, Janet just told me. I don't believe you took it."

"I didn't—"

She swallowed hard. "I really do like you, but don't come over. Your family will never accept me, and that's a lot of pressure I don't know how to handle." Rhee felt the uncertainty pulse within her veins. *He doesn't understand how dangerous I can be.*

"Janet and Brian are just kidding around," Jared started to get up, but Rhiannon gave him a light mental push back into his seat.

She was so sick with hurt that she could probably tear the whole school building down on top of Janet's blonde head and dance the Mambo while doing it. She whispered, "They're not funny." Then she turned on her heel, chin high, and walked out the door. *Please don't let me cry.*

Her mom showed up at the school fifteen minutes later. "Rhiannon, what's wrong?"

"I don't want to talk about it." Hanging on to her pride, and her out-of-control abilities, took all of her energy.

Her hands were full of books as they approached the van, so Rhee used her special power to open the door. Then she mentally slammed it shut behind her.

Her mom didn't say a word until they pulled into their driveway. Rhee jumped when Starla's hand settled on her shoulder.

"Honey? I can feel the confusion and the hurt coming from you like an open fire. Can't you tell me?"

She glanced at her mom from beneath her hair. Starla's blue eyes were swimming with unshed tears and her expression mirrored the sadness that Rhee felt deep inside. Her own tears slipped down her cheeks as she let go and sobbed the story of Brian and Janet, and how much she liked Jared, but they couldn't date, not when she wanted to physically harm Janet, and she finally confessed that she thought she might have made Janet's horse rear on purpose. Was she a horrible person? This wasn't the same as the Maddie Johnson situation, not even close. She hated being so out of touch with her emotions. *What happened to being able to make a logical decision?*

Her mom alternated from surprise, to disappointment, to pride. "You did the right thing, Rhiannon."

Did a girl ever get too old to need her mom?

As her mom hugged her tight, Rhee really, really hoped not.

Later, as she was curled up on the couch in front of a roaring fire in the giant fireplace, she realized that she'd been so *close* to happy. She'd truly tried to fit in. She'd joined stuff, made friends, done homework.

By the Goddess, she had pets.

Chewing her thumbnail, she adjusted the blanket over her legs. But she wasn't happy now, not at all.

Well, she was done trying to be something that she wasn't. She wanted to go back to Vegas. She had never been hurt like this when she'd been at the institute. Never. She'd been special. She'd been treated with respect.

Her mom came in with a tray of tea. "Here, honey. I wish your dad was here. He'd know what to do. Maybe he'd go over to the Roberts' house and kick that family in the butt, that's what!"

Rhee picked up a mug and hid a giggle. Her mom looked so funny when she was mad. "I just don't see Dad kicking someone's butt, Mom. Dad would talk and reason."

"Not when his baby girl is hurting, Rhee, I know that this is hard to hear right now, but heartache is natural and normal and...honey, it will get better with time."

Rhiannon rolled her eyes. "I like Jared, Mom. I'm sad because we won't get a chance to know each other better, but I can't trust myself to care for him. He could really hurt me."

Her mom arched an eyebrow.

"I'm withdrawing from the rodeo too. I don't need to humiliate myself anymore. I mean, it's obvious no matter what I do, people aren't going to like me."

"I'm not sure that's a good idea," her mom said with concern in her voice. "Quitting when things get rough isn't the way to build a stronger character."

Rhee bit her lip.

"I forgot! I was preparing the floor for the upstairs carpet today and I found a diary under your bed. I just thumbed through it, but it looks old. I thought you might want it, so I brought it downstairs. It will help get your mind off of what's-his-face. Now, where did I put it?"

Rhiannon watched with more than a little trepidation as her mom picked up cushions, peeked behind stacks of newspaper, and then peered beneath the couch. Was she ready to deal with Suzanne's problems?

Her mom stood and snapped her fingers. "I remember! Hang on."

Rhee heard the sound of the refrigerator door opening and then shutting.

Sure enough, when her mom handed her the book, it was cold. "The fridge?"

Her mom smiled. "You know how distracted I get. You called, and I must have stuck it in there before I left."

Rhee quickly dropped the book to her lap before she ended up in one of Suzanne's memories. "Thanks, Mom. I guess I'll read a little of it."

"Maybe there will be some history of the house in there."

"Yeah." *If only her mom knew.*

"If only fondue? Are you hungry, honey?"

Rhiannon shook her head as if her mom made perfect sense. "Huh uh."

Starla left the living room and Rhiannon picked up Suzanne's diary with the edge of the blanket.

To read, or not to read?

Well, she thought, *once I get Suzanne's mystery solved, then I can send her to the light and get back to Vegas where I belong. I might as well accomplish one thing I set out to do. And since I suck at fitting in the real world, that leaves me with banishing a one hundred-year-old ghost and her evil side-kick.*

Piece of cake.

She read. And she must have fallen asleep, since the sound of someone knocking on the door woke her up out of a deep dream.

Rubbing her eyes and smoothing her hair she thought, *Please don't be Jared. I can't take it anymore!*

Giggling. Her mom laughing. It was Melody and Bonnie. Rhiannon pushed back the blanket and got up, knocking the diary to the floor.

Suzanne might be a spirited ghost, but she sure had been a boring writer! Who cared about the voyage from England? Or dresses and gloves? Where was the good stuff? Like being in love, and her mom's illness?

She used her mind to shove the diary under the couch. Rhee wasn't quite ready to share Suzanne with her friends.

And Bonnie and Melody *were* her friends. When she went back to Vegas, she would probably miss them.

There was always email.

Her mom walked in, her bracelets practically singing. "Oh, good, Rhee, you're awake! Bonnie and Melody stopped by to see how you are. Isn't that sweet?"

Rhee nodded. "Sweet. Very. Hey, guys. Grab a seat."

Her mom left, and Melody sat on the opposite end of the couch from Rhiannon, while Bonnie took the stuffed chair across from them.

Bonnie blurted, "How are you? The school is buzzing with how you got into a big fight with Janet, and threatened to turn her into a toad. And you told Jared off. I thought you totally liked him!"

"She can't like someone who made a bet that he could hook up with her before the rodeo!" Melody said defensively.

Cheeks hot, Rhiannon said, "I am not turning Janet into a toad, and Jared didn't make any bet on hooking up with me— Janet was just trying to start trouble, as usual."

"I knew it," Bonnie punched the chair cushion. "I can't stand her."

Melody shrugged. "So you still like Jared?"

"Well, yes, but I really did tell him that I wouldn't date him."

"Explain?" Melody tapped her finger against her lower lip.

"If I dated Jared, I'd have to fight his entire family. I don't want to."

"If you really like him—"

Rhiannon compared the dull pain she felt all over to a bad toothache. "I don't like him that much," she lied to her friends.

Who, since they were her friends, totally saw right through the lie.

Bonnie slid her glasses up the bridge of her nose. "I was thinking. There has to be a way to get back at Janet."

"Yeah. Like how?"

"Well, the rodeo is a Crystal Lake tradition. The Roberts

family has always claimed founding the city of Crystal Lake. So, getting back at them through the rodeo sort of makes sense."

Melody slapped her knee. "Sabotage!"

Rhiannon rubbed her arms. Her friends had no idea the damage she could do if she wanted. "I don't know... People besides the Roberts could get hurt."

Bonnie exhaled with disappointment, "You're right. Never mind."

Melody giggled. "Don't give up yet. I have a great idea."

"You do?" Rhiannon wasn't sure she was up to Melody's great idea. The last time Rhee had seen the light bulb effect in Melody's eyes, Melody had ferreted out she was a Wiccan.

Bonnie grinned. "Tell!"

"How about something from Rhiannon's Book of Secrets?"

Bonnie sat back, her smile gone. "Witchcraft? Oh, I don't know, Melody. That might not be a good idea either. It would be better, I think, if we just put salt in the cotton candy machine."

Rhiannon agreed. "Listen, that magick stuff doesn't really work, right? I mean, I told you about how my dad was the one who really put the candy beneath my pillow."

Melody argued, "Witchcraft has been around forever. All those people can't be wrong. Maybe you just aren't doing the spells right."

"It doesn't matter; messing around with stuff you can't control is super dangerous." Rhiannon's arms were covered with goose bumps. *Her entire life was out of control!*

"Janet totally humiliated you today. She's been going around telling everyone that you are going to quit the challenge and run back to Vegas, where you belong."

Rhee felt the color flood her face, and she couldn't look at Melody.

"No way! Don't tell me you actually *are* running away?"

Rhiannon didn't like the guilt that spread through her system like a fever.

Bonnie said, "But you can't! You've been practicing so hard for the rodeo. And, well, you are incredible when it comes to not backing down from Janet. Don't let her get to you now—even if you don't win the bronco ride, at least you know that you stood up to her. I mean, *everybody* knows that you didn't do those posters."

Her friend's words were like a salve to her pride. But she was done—done! Janet had pushed her to the edge for the last time.

"In fact," Melody continued, "Jared is taking some serious heat from people who like you. They want to know what he did to upset you so bad. I saw him yelling at Janet, too, probably for spilling the beans about the bet."

Rhiannon squirmed on the couch. "He didn't take the bet."

"How can you know that?"

"I just do, Mel. He's not like the rest of his family."

"So we do something that doesn't hurt Jared," Melody pushed.

"I don't know, guys."

Bonnie stood; her face pale but determined. "If you can find a spell that will make Janet sick enough to make her miss the bronco ride, I think we should do it."

"Bonnie!" Rhiannon said, shocked. She'd been counting on Bonnie helping her hold out against Melody.

Melody jumped up and clapped. "Yahoo!"

Bonnie said, "It will be payback for every single thing she's ever done since kindergarten. Every time she stole my pink pencils, every time she pulled Melody's braids, made fun of

Corey, laughed at Meat and mocked Broomstick. She deserves to have something not go her way. Right?"

Rhiannon couldn't tell her friend no. What harm could be done? She hadn't been able to make a spell work, ever. And if by some piece of wild luck she could make it work, and Janet missed the rodeo...well, then Rhee could back out of the competition with no pressure. "I'll think about it."

Melody whistled. "Janet is goin' down!"

Chapter Twenty-Two

"I am so proud of you, Rhiannon Selene Godfrey. You are making the right choice by going back to school and facing Janet. And you-know-who. Here, put this in your pocket."

Rhiannon accepted the sachet of chamomile and fennel.

"To protect against harm," her mom told her. "Are you wearing your amulet?"

Rhiannon nodded and pulled out the crescent-shaped pendant from beneath her turtleneck sweater.

"Wonderful."

Rhee thought it was a little funny that her mom was so nervous for her. It actually calmed her down. "I'll be fine, Mom. Hey, is it okay if Bonnie and Melody sleep over tonight?"

"Are you sure that's a good idea, honey? Don't you want to be well rested for the rodeo tomorrow?"

"It'll be fun. I think I should focus more on that part than winning, don't you?"

Her mom beamed. "Of course, Rhiannon. Okay, let's go. You don't want to be late for school."

They weren't late, but Bonnie and Melody were already waiting for Rhiannon by the time the burgundy Celestial Beginnings van pulled up to the curb.

Rhee hustled over to join them before the bell rang. "Mom said you guys can stay over. Are you sure you want to do this?"

Melody was so excited she practically floated down the hall. "Oh, yeah. I checked the internet, and it will be a full moon tonight."

Great, Rhiannon thought. *Just when my supposed power will be at its strongest.* She had never told anybody, not even Matthew and Tanya, but her mom and dad had wanted a baby so bad, and they couldn't conceive. So they made a spring sacrifice to the Moon Goddess and, with the blessing of the Vegas Coven they'd belonged to, had performed a Great Rite.

Which resulted in Super-Psychic me.

"Helllooo, earth to Rhiannon!"

She blinked and said, "I was listening, Melody. Full moon."

"Cool. Janet's going to be sorry she messed with you. Do you have everything you need?"

"I guess. I looked through a few of the spells in my grimoire, but I didn't find anything. I quit writing in it years ago. I was just a kid."

"Well, I'm sure your mom has one."

"Melody, that would be like, I don't know, looking through somebody's underwear drawer."

Bonnie laughed. "Well, would she have just a regular book of spells?"

"I thought you hated witchcraft," Rhiannon whispered angrily.

Looking down her nose, Bonnie sniffed. "I am keeping an open mind."

"Okay, okay. I'll look before you guys get to my house. But remember, this is a secret."

The last thing she needed was for everyone at school to

think she was a witch. Which she wasn't. She didn't think.

Melody waved and went to her biology class while Bonnie and Rhee went in to math.

Jared tried to catch her eye as she made her way back to her seat, but Rhiannon refused to even glance at him. *If he smiles at me, I'm toast. I'll come up with a hundred reasons why we should hang out, and then his poisonous sister will come around and make me mad and I'll lose control of my temper and ruin everything.*

She kept her gaze straight ahead, but that didn't stop her from feeling his hurt.

It was awful.

Somehow that just made the plan to punish Janet less appealing. What if that thing with twins was true, and by making Janet sick, she'd make Jared sick too? By the time she got home from school, she felt like she might be the one to puke. But she couldn't let her new friends down, could she? No matter which choice she made, she was going to disappoint somebody. Even herself.

She sighed and logged on to the computer. She had three messages from Matthew.

She opened her email and read the one from yesterday.

Matthew: *I've been thinking about you a lot lately—miss you* ☹

Hmm, she thought as she bit her lower lip. Maybe Matthew realized what he'd let go by being so grown-up that he wouldn't even consider dating her.

The next message was from late last night.

Matthew: *Are you ok? Call me asap*

And the last message was from first thing this morning.

Matthew: *You could be in danger! Call me!!*

The hair on the back of her neck stood up. Danger? She and Matthew had never shared a telepathic link. They'd never shared anything other than a candy bar. In fact, Matthew had zero psychic skills other than the ever-useful fire-starting trick.

Laughing at that, she typed in a message telling him not to worry. She'd be back at the institute by Samhain. She yawned. Matthew was probably just overreacting because she hadn't talked to him in a while. She'd call later—after a little catnap.

She logged off and tripped over Suzanne's diary. "What the heck? I know I stuck you under the couch!"

Rhee glanced at the clock, realizing she had over an hour before her friends would show up. Sleep? Maybe she'd read a few more pages of the diary. She *had* ignored Suzanne.

She pulled the sleeves of her sweater down to use as gloves and grabbed the book. Snuggling on the couch, she turned to the last page she'd read before falling asleep. A nap sounded good, actually.

"Oh yeah. New gloves and hats." Rhiannon skimmed down the neatly scrawled handwriting, remembering that she'd never sent the diary to Tanya for a handwriting analysis.

"How could I have forgotten to do that?" she asked aloud. "How lame. I'm going to be the only fourteen-year-old Alzheimer's patient in the world."

She shook her head and read.

Dear Diary,

I have neglected you. But now Mother has died and Father has forbade my marriage. I only have you to turn to. Father is different since we buried Mother two months ago. His moods change like the weather. He won't listen to me when I say I love Adam, that once Adam and I are wed, he can come and live with us. Dearest Diary, it is as if he wants to stay in this house forever. I am too young to be locked away!

Rhiannon felt the chill all the way through her skin. Had Abediah locked Suzanne in the attic? She shivered and pulled the blanket around her legs. She'd wanted the good stuff, and here it was.

Finally, some answers. She turned to the next page.

Dear Diary,

I am meeting Adam tonight by the lake. I am going to convince him to wait for me. Father needs me, but I think that in the course of time, this need will lessen and he will move on. Perhaps even marry again. I cannot leave him while he is so distraught. Diary, I am worried that Adam will not wait much longer. He is an attractive man in need of a wife. I pray that he loves me enough to be patient.

Poor Suzanne! Rhiannon could feel her despair in the pages of the diary. There were a few more short entries and finally the last page.

Dear Diary,

Adam is dead. Father has lost his mind. I am all alone, with only you for a friend, though I won't be of this earth for much longer. I am shot and the wound is infected. Father won't get help, for how could he explain that it was he who shot me? It was an accident, I know, for I stepped in front of the second bullet meant for Adam. I have begged him to bring Doctor Mark, but he will not. With Adam deceased, it is as if one more murder, even of his daughter, would be nothing. I pray that God has mercy—

"That's it?" Rhiannon held the book upside down and shook it. "What happened to you, Suzanne?"

The spirit didn't answer, and suddenly Rhee wanted to know more than anything else in the world. The handwriting in the diary ended with a smear, like Suzanne had fallen asleep in mid-sentence. Or died.

One way to find out, Rhee thought with more than a little fear. She pulled the sweater from her hands and cautiously put her fingers on Suzanne's diary. The last entry, to be precise.

"Show me, Suzanne. Show me."

Wind blew around her face and the air grew heavy. It looked like heat coming off of a hot Las Vegas sidewalk, all shimmery, yet not there. Her senses sharpened and she could smell the dank interior of a closed space. Rotted wood. She felt the weight of loneliness and despair and fear wrap around her, sinking her backward in time.

She grasped the book and closed her fluttering eyes. Back, back, through darkness and pain. Her shoulder throbbed and her throat ached and scratched. Her body was so cold, so very cold, and she shuddered.

She turned, found herself on a small cot. The room was black as night with only a small candle flickering on a low table. Her lips were dry and cracked and she struggled to keep her eyes open.

"Father." Her voice was a whisper. Nobody answered and she slowly pushed herself from the cot. Another cot had been squeezed into the small area. Rhiannon-Suzanne shuffled over and looked down.

"Adam?" Suzanne asked hoarsely.

"I will kill him for hurting you."

A sharp pain in her upper arm made her gasp. *"No, Adam. It was my own fault, for stepping in front of the gun. I have asked him to bring Doctor Mark. Here, drink, just a bit."*

Rhiannon didn't fight Suzanne's body as they gave Adam a sip of water.

The water leaked from the corner of his mouth and his handsome brown eyes flashed with fever and fire. *"I am dying, Suzanne, but so will he!"*

"He thought that we were going to elope. He was frightened, Adam. He was afraid of being left alone. I told you he wasn't well. Father must have followed me out of the house. Adam, he dragged us both back here so that we could heal. Father won't let us die."

Suzanne's hand grasped Adam's and Rhiannon felt the heat of his illness sear her palm.

"No, Suzanne. He brought us back to this stinking attic so that we could die with no one the wiser. You can't see your father for the evil man he is."

"Adam!" Suzanne was sobbing. *"His mind was broken when my mother died. Theirs was a love as strong as ours. You must rest, Adam. My father is not evil."*

"I am dying, Suzanne. Your father will let us both rot in this attic. But don't worry, darling. I won't leave you alone. I will be with you, always. Get me a gun, and I will protect you from your father. From everyone who would stand in our way."

Adam coughed and Suzanne wiped his forehead with a handkerchief. Suddenly he raised his head from the cot and shouted, *"You are mine, Suzanne!"*

Then he fell back and Rhiannon knew he was dead. She shared the tears that flowed thickly down Suzanne's cheeks. She shared the sadness of losing a loved one, and the pain of Suzanne's fever that raged through her veins.

Suzanne shuffled back to her own cot and lay down, coughing and spluttering and crying. The pain was horrible. Overwhelming. Rhiannon didn't think she could survive it. Was this how Suzanne died, alone in a dark attic with no company save a dead man?

Rhiannon wanted out.

Would she die with Suzanne? She struggled to get free of Suzanne's memories. The young woman ignored her, and Rhee started to panic.

Let me go, let me go. I don't want to die. She rocked back and forth on the cot, in Suzanne's body, trapped. She yelled as loudly as she could, *"Suzanne! Suzanne!"*

"Wake up, Rhiannon!"

Her mom tapped her cheeks with her fingers. "Honey, wake up! Who is Suzanne? Why are you crying?"

Rhiannon sat up, shaking and terrified, certain she had been about to die.

"By the Goddess, you're bleeding!"

Chapter Twenty-Three

"It isn't blood. It can't be." Rhiannon had never been so scared in her life. She checked her shoulder for a wound, but there wasn't one. But the red gooey stuff, which looked like blood, was exactly in the spot that Suzanne had been shot.

"Does it hurt?"

"No, Mom."

Rhiannon wiped tears from her cheeks, thinking of Suzanne, who had been kept a prisoner with her dead fiancé in the attic upstairs. Abediah Roberts had been a murderer. Something that the Roberts family had covered up quite nicely with the story about Suzanne eloping with her fiancé, Adam.

All lies. It was obviously a genetic trait throughout the family tree. She shivered and her mom pulled her into a hug.

"Oh, honey. You have me so worried. I don't know what to do. I think we should fly to Vegas, make an appointment with Dr. Richards."

"Mom, calm down. I can explain, kinda. The nightmare was caused by the diary." Sort of. "Suzanne Roberts's diary."

Her mom arched a brow. "What? As in the Roberts who founded Crystal Lake?"

"Uh huh. It turns out that Abediah murdered his daughter, but Jared told me, in their version of family history, that

Suzanne had run away and gotten married."

Starla plopped down on the floor. "That would be enough to bring on nightmares. But the blood?"

Rhiannon shrugged, scared enough to be honest with her mom. "I don't know. Suzanne had been shot."

Her mom buried her head in the blanket and muttered, "In the shoulder, right?"

"Yeah." Rhee tried to smile. "Just another new psychic phenomenon."

Her mom raised her face, which was pale and worried and filled with love. "Is there anything else I should know? No matter what the problem is, we'll get through it."

The knocking on the front door broke the mom-daughter moment, and Rhee was grateful. Any more of that bonding junk and she'd spill her guts about everything.

She ran to the door and answered it. "C'mon in!"

"What's on your sweater?" Melody asked.

"Mmm, ketchup. I'll go and change in a sec. Hey! Where are your glasses, Bonnie?"

Bonnie fluttered her lashes. "Contact lenses. Mom surprised me with them when I got home. And a new pair of jeans too. They actually fit."

She twirled on the front porch while Rhiannon and Melody laughed.

"You look great!" Rhee said. Maybe today was the day for mom-daughter make-up. She glanced at Melody, who was happy, but not. Like, trying to be happy on the outside, but underneath a little... Rhiannon concentrated as she stared at her friend. Jealous.

Jealous? Melody never talked about her dad, rarely about her mom, and mostly about her grandmother. Someday she'd have to figure out why.

Melody snapped, "Stop analyzing me, Rhee. I'm fine."

Taken back, Rhiannon wondered if maybe Melody had more than a few psychic bones in her body.

She put her arm around Bonnie. "You look like a million. Are you going to get Corey to buy you a Coke tomorrow at the rodeo?"

"Corey doesn't care about me. He's funny and wonderful and—" her voice dropped to a whisper as they walked into the house, "—and Rhee, I was going to ask you to make me a love spell."

Rhiannon stopped so fast that Melody bumped into her back.

Bonnie waved her hand in the air, as if erasing what she'd said. "But then...then I wouldn't know whether or not Corey liked me because he liked me, or whether or not it was magick."

Rhiannon's shoulders slumped with relief. "Good thinking, Bon. I don't know any love spells, anyway."

"Did you find a spell book?"

"Um, no. I...fell asleep."

Melody snorted. "You sure take a lot of naps."

Rhiannon wasn't about to tell them that psychic experiences made her as sleepy as a baby, in addition to thirsty. "So I like my sleep. Hey, how about you guys go ask my mom to show you the furniture she's got for her shop, and then I'll go look through her bookshelves."

Melody and Bonnie set out to find Starla and Rhiannon ran upstairs. She pulled book after book down. Hmm, she thought: *Wicca and Witchcraft for the Initiated Witch.* Maybe. That one had possibilities. Didn't they make a witchcraft and spell manual for dummies?

She was so busy trying to find the right book that Suzanne scared her to pieces.

"Don't do this thing, Rhiannon."

"Suzanne! Sheesh, can't you wear a bell or something?" Rhiannon put her hand over her heart, which was thumping so hard it hurt.

"This is not safe. When you open the door between the worlds, other spirits may enter. Spirits you cannot control."

"I don't plan on opening any doors. Magick doesn't really work. It is the *belief* that makes a spell happen. And since I don't really believe, well...the spell is bound to fail. I'm only doing this to make Bonnie and Melody happy."

"Rhiannon. You are so naïve."

"Me? Whatever! I know all about you now. You are stuck in this house with your father. He was crazy, and Mrs. Edwards said that crazy people and teens have the highest psychic reception."

Suzanne laughed. It was a sad, brittle sound.

"Rhiannon. Don't do this. You will be sorry, and once something is done it cannot be undone."

The spirit faded away as her mom and her friends came back inside.

"Shh!" Rhiannon whispered as she led the way out to the pasture through the laundry room.

Melody covered her mouth with her hand to smother a nervous giggle.

Bonnie shut the door quietly behind them.

They tiptoed, even when they were on the grass. Finally, they were in the middle of the pasture. The moon was bright and Rhiannon felt an unexpected jolt of mystical power as the moonbeams splashed her face.

It was weird, an omen, maybe and she turned to face her friends. "Okay. Are you sure, sure, sure you want to do this?"

Melody answered impatiently. "Yes!"

Bonnie blinked, her eyes bright green and clear without her glasses. "We aren't going to hurt her, right? Just make her sick so that she misses her chance to ride."

"Nobody is going to get hurt. In fact, one of the spells we could do would just stop Janet from being mean and spiteful." Thank the Goddess she'd found that one!

"How is that going to help you win the rodeo thing tomorrow?"

"Melody, I've told you a zillion times that I don't care about winning. I just want Janet to stop thinking she can mess with us"

"I think we need to make her sick. Like, with the chicken pox or something."

Rhiannon shook her head. "I definitely don't know how to do that."

Bonnie said, "Let's just do the one that will make her quit being mean, then."

Melody exhaled. "You guys are babies."

"There can't be any negativity in the circle, Melody. We have to be at peace with one another. We have to focus on our goal, and be one with it."

Bonnie crossed her arms. "Okay."

Melody sighed. "All right. No negativity."

Rhiannon took her notes out of her bag. Then she handed

the school picture of Janet to Bonnie, and the white candle in a silver holder to Melody.

"I will light the candle, and we'll hold hands around it. We need to think only about Janet. I wrote this, supposedly rhyming chants help, so it isn't, like, great, or anything, but it should get what we want across. Ready?"

Her friends nodded.

"Repeat after me: No harm to thee, just calm and peace. Your spite and anger must hereby cease."

Melody huffed. "Definitely not poet of the year material."

Bonnie elbowed her in the waist. "Positive energy."

The girls repeated the chant three times, then Rhiannon took the picture of Janet and set it in the flames.

"No harm to thee, just calm and peace, your spite and anger must hereby cease."

One minute Rhiannon was really getting into it, feeling peace, feeling calm, feeling good.

The next minute it was like someone turned on a huge fan from a movie set.

A strong wind stormed around them from nowhere and Bonnie screamed as it tore at her hair. Melody was knocked to the grass as if pushed by a giant hand and Rhiannon did her best to stand her ground against the invasive, invisible force. Danger pulsed around her.

She instinctively held out her arms and raised her eyes to the moon. Bonnie was huddled like a turtle in her shell and Melody had crawled over to protect her. Rhee shouted to be heard over the surging gusts, "Rhiannon, Moon Goddess, my namesake! Protect us from this evil!"

A black cloud came between her and the bright moon. It was suddenly dark as black paint and Rhiannon was momentarily blinded.

Doubt and anger and fear overwhelmed her as she trembled in the night, beneath the dark. Bonnie whimpered as the wind howled and she knew she never should have tried to do this. Her friends were at risk. Suzanne had tried to warn her.

Rhiannon yelled, "Abediah! Be gone from here!"

Malevolent laughter as evil and thick as sludge raced across her skin and she shuddered with nausea. A deep, husky voice rasped out, *"You know nothing! Nothing. I need your energy, Rhiannon Godfrey. I want your life force! You shouldn't have interfered with what was mine. Give me your breath!"*

Rhiannon felt the air being sucked from her lungs. She was going to lose, she was going to die, and it was all her own fault.

Then a voice yelled, "Be GONE!"

The cloud of black dissipated as if it had never been and the moon shone twice as bright. The wind stopped so quickly Rhiannon stumbled.

Her mother stood, tall and furious, in a white nightgown. Her feet were bare, her red hair was wild and she looked like an avenging goddess.

"Rhiannon Selene, gather your friends. *You* must close the circle. Now."

Melody got to her feet, trembling, then helped Bonnie to stand. Bonnie was crying and shaking.

"I'm so sorry," Rhee said over and over again.

Starla herded them into a circle around the candle and prayed for the Goddess's forgiveness. She forced Rhiannon to perform the rites, and then she ordered them all into the house and demanded to know what *exactly* had been going on.

"Rhiannon. I am so disappointed in you. You know that you should never meddle with another's life."

Her mom's mouth was wrinkled with disapproval as she added sternly, "After what happened with Maddie Johnson, I sincerely thought you had learned your lesson."

Melody asked, "Who is Maddie?"

Starla tapped her toe against the kitchen floor. "Answer them."

Rhiannon blinked back tears. "First, I want to say that I am sorry. I never should have risked playing with something I don't understand, or—" she glanced at her mom, remembering the mystical pull of the moon, "—appreciate."

Her mom kept tapping her toe.

Rhee bit her lip and welcomed the painful memory. "Maddie Johnson was a girl my own age who moved into our apartment building last year. I hurt her. On purpose."

Her friends were silent, and non-judgmental. "When she first came, I was so excited. I mean, I thought that we'd be friends. Only, it turned out that she wasn't my friend. At all."

Rhiannon wiped her nose with the back of her hand. She was crying freely, she couldn't help it, recalling what Maddie had done. And yes, what she had done in return.

"She told everyone in the building that my mom and dad were witches. That they sacrificed babies at midnight and worshipped the devil. I mean, Mr. Finklestien, the doorman, wouldn't even open the door for me anymore, he was so scared. Maddie lied to all the tenants; she told them to be careful. That my parents had a list with everybody's name on it, and they could be the next victim if they made the Godfreys angry."

Her mom blinked. "What?"

"I never told you the real reason behind what I did, because I knew that you would have said that they were 'just words' and I should ignore them. But Mom, I had showed Maddie my grimoire; I had invited her into our house. You were my parents, and I had given her the tools to ruin your reputations."

Rhee paused. "We'd argued and Maddie wouldn't take back the things she had said. So I—" she took a deep breath and then said quickly, "—I pushed her down the stairs and made her hair fall out."

Bonnie's eyes popped open. "No way."

Melody's jaw dropped. "Cool!"

Starla wiped the tears from her cheeks. "Rhee."

Rhiannon continued, and it felt kinda good to finally admit what she had done. She'd been blaming Maddie for everything for so long, it was a relief. The next words were harder to say, but she had to. "So, it is all my fault that we had to move here from Vegas. My parents gave up everything they loved so that I could have a fresh start."

Melody shuffled her feet. "I guess we shouldn't have talked you into it, doing the spell."

"You didn't talk me into anything. I am way old enough to make my own choices, and what I did was stupid. But, Mom, I swear that we didn't do a harming spell. I used a banishing spell, so that Janet wouldn't be mean."

Her mom hugged her close. "Any time you open yourself to magick, there is the potential of it going wrong. Did you do a protective ring of sea salt? No. Did you do an herbal smudging? No. You left yourself wide open to danger."

Melody asked, "What happened? What was that wind thing?"

Starla stepped back, but kept her hand on Rhee's arm. "Yes, Rhiannon. Why don't you tell us what that was?"

Rhiannon swallowed, and knew the time for certain secrets was over. She couldn't tell her mom everything, not with Melody and Bonnie present.

And she couldn't tell Melody and Bonnie most of it. She was still keeping her psychic talents to herself. Suzanne's diary was a safe enough bet and maybe her friends wouldn't completely freak out when she shared her theory. She could only try.

"Not what." She told them in a matter-of-fact voice. "*Who.* Abediah Roberts."

Chapter Twenty-Four

The morning sun was bright as it fell on Rhiannon's face. She woke up, blinked, and looked around. Bonnie and Melody were all tangled up in blankets on the living room floor, but her mom was awake and sitting on the couch.

"How do you feel, Rhiannon?"

"Better. Thanks, Mom."

"I've been thinking about this all night. It wasn't your fault that we moved." She patted the couch next to her. "Come sit, honey. You know we just wanted you to have a chance to be a regular kid."

Rhiannon sat, worried that her mom was gonna be all emotional again. Rhee hadn't got much sleep last night, thinking about who she was and the problems she had to face. Her mom and her friends had really been there for her, and she knew, in her heart, that she wouldn't be a stinking pariah if Bonnie and Melody ever found out about her psychic abilities. They'd taken the Roberts' ghost, and the *possibly* haunted farmhouse, in stride. She leaned into her mom.

Starla said, "But you aren't *regular* at all. You are special. You have an incredible gift."

Rhee patted her mom's hand, hating that her eyes were getting all watery.

"We took you away from the institute because we were afraid that you used your power to harm Maddie out of spiteful anger. If only you had told us the real reason, we would have understood you had been reacting with your heart. We definitely wouldn't have made you send her a get well card every day while she was recovering."

Rhee giggled, but her mom was on a roll. "And I know that I, personally, wouldn't have made her soup or brought flowers, or...or..."

Her mother's anger was gone as fast as it had arrived. She hugged Rhee close. "You still would have had to buy the poor girl a wig. Really, Rhiannon, causing all that child's hair to fall out. Mr. Finklestien thought we sacrificed babies? I am so glad that we sold our apartment. Those uneducated people! We lived there for over ten years. I love you, honey."

Rhiannon sniffed. "C'mon Mom. No more mushy stuff. I can't handle it today, okay? I know you want me to be normal, and I'm not."

"You're wrong, honey. We want you to be *you*." She clapped her hands together. "All right, enough of that. How about checking out the new clothes I bought you for your Rodeo Debut?"

"New clothes? Bring 'em on!"

Bonnie and Melody sat up and rubbed their eyes. Bonnie grumbled, "Clothes? Where? I'm blind."

Melody snickered. "Go put your eyes in so that we can see Rhee's new duds."

Starla stood. "Not just for Rhiannon. I bought shirts for you two, as well."

Rhiannon groaned. "We're not gonna look like the Three Musketeers are we? And no fringe, right, Mom?"

"No fringe."

A half hour later they all met downstairs in the living room.

Melody grabbed Rhiannon and sent her into a four-square spin. Bonnie caught her other arm and spun her back.

"We look *good*. Even if I fall off the bronco in two seconds and get stomped beneath the front hooves, at least I'll have died making a *killer* fashion statement."

Melody laughed. "Black jeans with silver studs, black cowboy boots with silver thread, and a red shirt with pearl buttons."

"Don't forget the silver bolo tie!" Bonnie flipped it up and Rhee snickered. Her mom figured if she could keep her daughter covered in enough silver, it would have to have some kind of magickal protection.

"If only Tanya could see me now. She'd laugh so hard her head would fall off."

"I like mine! That was so cool of your mom to get us shirts too. I love new clothes."

"Yeah," Bonnie added, "and she got me the right size."

The fairgrounds were already crowded when they got there, and for once Rhee didn't fuss about arriving in the Celestial Beginnings van. She asked for the tenth time, "Mom, Dad promised he'd be here, right?"

"Yep. He'll be here to watch you ride the bucking bronc. Since he's the only one who knows how to work the digital camera, he'd better show up. Why don't you girls go wander, and I'll get you checked in. Meet me at the corral in half an hour?"

"Okay."

Rhiannon knew she was gawking, but it was like she was in a time warp or something. She could easily see Suzanne in a setting just like this one. Everything was country and old-fashioned, and for once she saw the appeal.

"Nervous?" Melody asked.

"A little. Actually, after what happened last night, I am feeling much better about everything. I've never told anybody about Maddie before. It's embarrassing, you know?"

"You were trying to protect your parents, that's all," Bonnie said loyally.

"You know, if Janet is still mean after all this, I think we should tell everybody that good old Abediah Roberts was a killer. That would set the whole family back on their tails."

Rhiannon lightly punched Melody in the arm. "No way, José. I'm done meddling. And you promised to keep it secret."

"Whatever." Melody walked a little faster. "It's nice to know that you have an ace up your sleeve, just in case."

"Why do you hate them so bad? It's more than Janet pulling your braids, isn't it?"

Melody shrugged.

Bonnie blabbed. "Melody's mom used to work for Mr. Roberts at the feed store, until his wife, Mrs. Roberts, fired her. For being beautiful. Mrs. Roberts was jealous, plain and simple."

"Bonnie!" Melody's brown eyes flashed. "You said you wouldn't say anything!"

Bonnie patted her arm. "Everybody knows. Wouldn't you rather Rhiannon hear it from us? We're friends. Friends don't need to keep secrets."

Rhiannon winced. She still had plenty of things to hide. She understood all about secrets. "I'll stop pestering you with questions."

Pausing, Melody kicked a decorative bale of hay. "Don't you

Her Wiccan, Wiccan Ways

want to hear the rest?"

"Um. Only if you want to tell me?"

Melody was angry, an emotion that Rhiannon recognized, no prob.

"So now my mom is a bar maid in Tilton, thirty miles away, and my dad left us over a year ago. Supposedly to find work, but he ain't comin' back."

Rhiannon didn't know what to say, so she looked at Bonnie, who had obviously decided she'd said enough.

Taking a deep breath, Rhee commiserated. "You're right. It sucks. But none of that is *your* fault. You are great, and pretty, and smart. Ten times better than Janet. I'm sorry about your dad. Maybe he'll come back, right? But you still have your mom, even if she does have to work so hard. And your grandma. And us."

Rhiannon pointed between herself and Bonnie.

Melody planted her hands on her hips. "Listen, Oprah, I don't want to talk about it anymore. But the next time I need cheering up, I'll give you a call. And as for you, Bonnie, I guess I won't kill you. Oh, man, don't turn around."

Rhee did. "What?"

"I said not to turn, but there's Jared, totally staring at you."

Rhiannon shrugged, even though her stomach muscles tightened into a ball. "What do I care about that?"

Bonnie said, "He looks like he wants to talk to you. He's coming this way."

She had to ask, since she had turned back, "Is he with Janet?" Some of the whole acknowledging-your-faults thing had made her re-think the Janet fiasco too. After the rodeo, she had plans to make a lot of stuff right.

Melody shook her head. "Nah. He's with two of his buds,

though. Caleb and some other guy. You want to talk?"

Rhiannon had to concentrate on being able to stay on her horse. Not Jared. Her epiphany didn't change the Roberts' hate for her. "Huh-uh. Maybe after the ride. We'll see."

Melody smiled. "Then let's go find out when you ride."

"All right." The three linked arms and walked in companionable silence until they reached the corral. The horses were wild-eyed and Rhiannon grinned. "You know, I think I'm really excited about this."

"I think you're crazy," said a male voice behind her. She spun around and there was Matthew. She threw her arms around him and gave him a huge hug. "How did you get here?"

"I brought him."

"Tanya!"

"In the flesh."

"But your mom..."

Her friend smiled and winked. "Your dad can be pretty persuasive."

"Dad?"

"Right here, Rhee."

"Man, I feel like I'm stuck in *The Wizard of Oz*. I'm Dorothy and all these people keep popping up!"

"Well, then, how about a welcome for us too?"

Rhiannon kissed her dad on the cheek before turning around. "Dr. Richards? Mrs. Edwards? *Wow!*"

She was so happy that she hugged them both at the same time. Looking into Dr. Richards' familiar eyes she said, "We have *got* to talk."

He leaned down to whisper so that her dad wouldn't hear what he had to say. "I know it, young lady. I know it. I was wondering how long it would take before you would realize what you were up against."

Rhiannon froze and flicked a glance toward her parents. "Matthew told?"

"Oh, no, luv," said Mrs. Edwards. "I have been in contact with Suzanne since you moved in."

Rhiannon sputtered, sure she hadn't heard right.

"Oh, no, dear. You heard me correctly." The medium winked.

"But I thought I was doing this on my own."

Her dad came over, cleared his throat and patted her on the shoulder. "You're up, Rhee."

They quickly got her into her helmet and her pads and the next thing she knew she was sitting on top of a bucking bronco in a stall that was barely big enough to hold them both. She looked out and saw her friends and family staring over the fence and cheering.

Excitement buzzed through her as she wrapped her gloved hands around the reins. "Please, Goddess, just don't let me, like, die, or anything."

The stall door opened and out she went. She was flying and hanging on for dear life and laughing with the thrill of it—and then she was *really* flying as the horse bested her and bucked her off.

She landed in a pile of straw and quickly ran up the fence just as she'd been taught.

The announcer yelled, "Rhiannon Godfrey, five seconds!"

Melody climbed up next to her. "That was wild!"

Bonnie said, "Janet's best time last year is twelve. Are you okay?"

Rhiannon laughed and laughed. "I can't *wait* to do that

again!"

Janet was next and Rhiannon, in her heart, wished her the best of luck. Not that Janet needed it; she turned out to be really talented.

The announcer yelled, "Janet Roberts! Crystal Lake's Champion for three years running, fourteen seconds!"

Rhiannon found herself clapping along with the crowd. They all stayed and watched until the end of the event, chattering and just having fun. Later, Janet rode around the corral holding her trophy. She trotted right by Rhiannon and said, "Not bad for a city girl, Rhiannon."

Rhiannon smiled. It was good enough for her.

They spent the rest of the day at the rodeo, and Rhiannon managed to avoid Jared for most of it. It was hard not to sneak peeks at him when he walked by. Even harder not to search for him in the crowd. What was her problem?

Why did she have to still have a crush on a guy who she knew wasn't good for her? And she certainly wasn't good for him.

She was hopeless.

Walking arm in arm with Matthew and Tanya, Bonnie and Melody, she enjoyed the rustic fair…they even all participated in an apple-dunking contest.

"Your mom would die if she saw you eating apples that other people could have touched, Tanya," Rhiannon teased.

"Yeah, well, she isn't here, so I get to live dangerously!"

She couldn't believe it when it was time to leave. Melody's grandma came to pick up Melody and Bonnie, while everyone else piled into the minivan. It felt right, bringing her old friends further into her new life.

She knew from the way her dad kept shooting glances at

her that her mom had blabbed about the spell thing last night. And from his hug that her mom hadn't left out any of the cryin' stuff, either. Her parents were pretty all right, and yet she was still lying to them.

Her stomach clenched tight. A lie by omission was still a lie, right? And she'd kept Suzanne a secret long enough, as well as the crazy idea that she could banish the evilness from the farmhouse by herself.

They pulled up the gravel drive and Mrs. Edwards grasped Matthew's hand.

"Oh, my." The medium closed her eyes. "The danger here is very strong."

Matthew glared at Rhiannon. "I told you to call me—I knew there was trouble."

Actually, she'd completely forgotten Matthew's earlier email warning. "How'd you know about that?" Rhee asked. "Never mind, just remember that my parents don't know about Suzanne being a *ghost*."

Her mom got out of the van and shut the door, then she marched up the stairs and stood on the porch with her hands on her hips. She waited until everyone was out of the vehicle and gathered below the stairs to the house before saying, "Rhiannon, I don't know how much of a ditz you take me for. But I am perfectly aware of the ghosts. You didn't really think your father and I bought that goat story, did you?"

Rhiannon sucked in a breath. "You knew?"

Her dad answered, "Not at first, but we've been in touch with Dr. Richards via email and phone. We tried to get you to admit you needed help, but you *are* stubborn. I think you get that from your mom's side of the family."

"Miles! Your area rug was perfectly fine, Rhee. We just had to think of something to keep you from your room—a delayed carpet was the best I could come up with."

"Thanks, Mom." Rhiannon wasn't sure whether to be relieved that her secret was out in the open or disappointed that she hadn't banished the spirit herself. "Mrs. Edwards?"

The Irish medium said, "You were very close to helping Suzanne, Rhiannon. It was the dark spirit upstairs that came as a nasty surprise to us. Suzanne didn't know how to communicate what was happening, and while your gift is strong, it needs to be trained. Untrained mediums can cause damage to themselves and to those around them." She lowered her voice, "There is no harm in asking for help, luv. There are times when you can do more harm if you don't."

Rhiannon blushed and Matthew put his arm around her shoulders. "I overheard Doc and Mrs. Edwards talking about you and Suzanne last night and knew the jig was up. When I found out that they were coming here with your dad, I invited myself."

"Ah, that explains your cryptic email."

"We were very disappointed that Matthew hadn't shared your secret." Dr. Richards sent each of them a look. "There could have been trouble."

Rhee glanced around her, making sure to include everyone when she confessed, "I guess I wanted to impress all of you. So that you would want me to come back to the institute. I want to be a parapsychologist."

Dr. Richards dipped his head. "I know. Your parents know too. But they were right in forcing you to be with other kids. To broaden your horizons! Haven't you enjoyed your time here?"

Rhiannon hated to admit it. "Well, yeah."

"You've made friends?"

"Uh-huh. But I still want to be—"

Her dad interrupted, "We've worked out a compromise, Rhee, if you want. You can spend summers with Dr. Richards, and maybe a few weekends during the year. If you really try to make things work out here."

"Daddy!" Rhiannon ran to him and gave him a hard hug. Then she waved at her mom, who was smiling from her spot before the door. "You guys are the best."

He rocked back on his heels with a smug look. "We are pretty cool."

Mrs. Edwards cleared her throat. "Well. If we could go inside now, I believe we can free a tormented spirit. I'll lead, and you can follow, Rhiannon."

This was everything she'd wanted. Almost. As she looked around at her friends and family, she knew it beat the heck out of being scared and alone. Maybe she really was starting to grow up.

Chapter Twenty-Five

"I'll miss Suzanne when she's gone," Rhiannon said.

"I don't believe you will." Mrs. Edwards winked and chuckled.

"Huh? Aren't you sending her to the light?"

"She doesn't wish to go. Every powerful medium has a spirit guide. And Suzanne wants to be yours."

Rhiannon was both happy and confused at the same time. She hadn't thought about being a medium. How cool was that? "How come you can talk to Suzanne? She said she couldn't leave the house."

"Then who saved you in the barn? Or got your mother to come out to the pasture?"

Suzanne had really been yakking Mrs. Edwards' ears off. Rhee crossed her arms over her chest. "I don't understand."

"At first I mind-traveled to Suzanne, but she's learning too. She just needed a medium to connect with outside her known boundaries. It takes training, dearie. I'll be working with you both, but for now, what you need to know is that we are banishing Adam Miller. *He* is the angry spirit who has tried to keep Suzanne trapped inside the farmhouse, not Abediah. She loved him, once, before he let his anger turn him toward darkness." The medium gave Rhee a calculating look. "Sound familiar?"

Rhiannon leaned against the doorway, kinda sick and very surprised. "No way! Adam?" She remembered the strong emotions he'd had before he died. Of course, she could see how being murdered when you were supposed to elope might do that to a guy. "I should have realized. She even showed me in her memory, when he said he wouldn't ever leave her."

Mrs. Edwards smiled. "Suzanne says that in life Adam was quick tempered, and stubborn too. He refused to pass over when he died, honoring his vow to stay with Suzanne. By the time Suzanne herself passed a week later, Adam was furious at Abediah and wouldn't let Suzanne go to the light. He trapped her in this house and haunted Abediah, who had gone to get the doctor and fallen in a ditch, breaking his leg. Finally, Abediah decided to leave the farm behind. He built a new homestead and started his life over."

"But how did Suzanne get away from him at all?"

"Adam's bursts of fury were short and left him tired, so she was able to break free every once in a great while. And she couldn't allow him to hurt you."

Dr. Richards patted her back. "You have a lot of natural skill, young lady. And a lot to learn."

"What was the black stuff? Does it mean that I will turn out to be bad?"

The doctor scratched his ear. "That is a lesson that will take some time. Everybody has the potential to be good or bad. You, Rhiannon, are good. We need to work on your temper, but ..."

Matthew gave her a playful push inside the house. "Rhiannon needs a time out!"

Rhiannon pushed back, the lesson pushed aside. "Do not!"

"Do, too."

"Hey!"

Tanya wrapped her arms around both of them. "Man, have I missed this. All we need is some chips."

"You ate chips at the institute?" Starla tapped her foot and glared at Dr. Richards.

The man shrugged and stepped behind Mrs. Edwards, who didn't bother hiding a grin.

"So, are we going to do, like, a séance?" Rhee rubbed her arms.

Mrs. Edwards clicked her teeth. "Let me see if I can communicate with Adam one on one. Where is the greatest source of power?"

"The closet!" Rhee and her mom answered at the same time.

"You knew?" Rhiannon yelled.

Her mom's bracelets jingled nervously. "I had your father paint and build new shelves. I was trying to block the negative energy. I even mixed lavender oil with the paint. We had no idea how bad it was going to get, since you didn't *tell* us."

Dr. Richards' eyebrows flew up. "Hmm. Lavender oil. Interesting."

Starla went up another stair. "You know, a séance isn't that different from a witching circle."

Rhiannon figured if Dr. Richards' brows moved up any farther then they'd just fall off his face. "Hmm. Yes. There certainly are some similarities."

"I think I just said so."

Her dad pulled her mom faster up the stairs and pushed open the door to Rhiannon's room.

Mrs. Edwards stopped and held out her palms. "Oh, my. He's very angry, isn't he, Rhiannon?"

Rhee took a hesitant breath. "My shields haven't been working so well. To tell the truth, something I haven't been doing a lot of lately, but I *so* plan on changing... I'm kind of afraid of being in here."

Matthew snorted. "I was expecting a real confession. Something we all didn't know, dork."

When Tanya didn't laugh, Rhiannon looked for her friend and found her near the hatbox. "Oh, don't touch that. It's powerful."

Tanya didn't seem to hear her. Rhee looked at Mrs. Edwards, who was simply watching what Tanya did next.

Apprehension soared around the room. Rhee froze. Being worried didn't usually make the curtains dance, or...the jewelry box crash to the ground. "No! Tanya, watch out!"

Her friend was surrounded by the black essence. It swirled and seemed to suck at Tanya's skin, bleaching her friend to a skeleton color. Rhee tried to run toward Tanya, but Mrs. Edwards grabbed her. "Wait, Rhiannon. Watch."

The eerie essence started to take on a solid shape and Rhee could see the shadow of a man take over the body of her friend. "Tanya?"

"She can't hear you," Mrs. Edwards said gently.

"Bring her back!"

"She's been trained to do this, with help, of course. She volunteered to come."

"I don't care!" Rhee panicked.

The shape became more solid, so that less of Tanya was visible. It was weird, like seeing a holographic picture. Parts of Tanya, parts of Adam Miller, depending on how you tilted your head to look.

Matthew shook his head in wonder. "Wow. I mean, we talked about her trying this, but I didn't realize."

The figure of Adam Miller laughed. "Come here. I can show you how it's done, boy."

Mrs. Edwards stepped forward. "Enough. Tanya has allowed you to use her body to communicate. Rhiannon doesn't understand that her shields were the only things keeping you all the way out of her body. You are an evil thing, Adam Miller, and it is time for you to move on."

"I am happy here," he said. Rhee noticed the figure didn't move his lips, but Tanya did, when he spoke.

"Nonsense." Mrs. Edwards snapped her fingers as Dr. Richards pointed at Tanya's figure, which was starting to slump.

"She's weakening," he mumbled.

Mrs. Edwards held out her hands. "Matthew, Rhiannon, Mr. and Mrs. Godfrey, please help us create a circle around Tanya."

Rhee was proud of her mom as Starla didn't even question the medium but grabbed her dad's hand and then Matthew's.

"Adam, you are not wanted in this house. We banish you. Suzanne does not love you anymore, and so we banish you."

The shape started to dissolve. "No!"

The medium kept her eyes closed as she said, "You may have loved Suzanne at one time, but you care for nothing but gaining power. You want shape. You want life. You must go through the cycle like everyone else. Death to rebirth, Adam. We banish you."

"Nooo!"

Rhee held her breath as the eerie not-there shadowy being

flickered stronger, then weaker.

Mrs. Edwards said again, only this time her mom and dad joined her, "We banish you!"

Soon they were all chanting and Rhiannon could feel the force of their joined hands, could feel the power of both the psychic and the magick combined. Was there room in her for both?

"We banish you!"

With a loud pop, the essence of Adam Miller was gone. Dr. Richards ran to Tanya, who blinked her eyes and stood straight. "Freaky! Did I do it? Did I?"

Mrs. Edwards started to laugh. "Yes, luv. You certainly did."

Rhee put her hands on her hips. "I thought that Matthew was training with you, Mrs. Edwards. Why didn't he help?"

Mrs. Edwards shrugged sadly. "Matthew hasn't this gift. He's chosen another way to use his abilities."

Rhee felt Matthew's hurt when she turned to him. "What are you going to do? There isn't much money in being a fire-starter. In fact, most people call them arsonists and they end up in jail."

Matthew smiled sadly. "Way to cut to the core of the matter. I'm thinking of leaving the institute."

Rhiannon's world dropped out from underneath her. "But...you can't!"

Dr. Richards and Mrs. Edwards exchanged a cryptic look before he dropped his hand on Matthew's shoulder. "We're doing our best to talk him into staying, Rhiannon. Maybe you could help."

Matthew sighed. "Thanks a lot."

Starla made tea, one of her favorite things to do for a

crowd, and they all settled in front of the large fireplace that had become the center of the Godfrey home. Of course, when a girl drank a lot of tea, it required a few trips to the bathroom.

Rhiannon was on her way back to join her friends when she heard a knock on the door. She peeked out the window, wondering who could be at her house since it was getting kinda late.

She didn't see anybody, but opened the door anyway. Had she heard someone saying her name?

"Rhee?" her mom called.

Not you, Mom. "I'll be right there," she yelled back, and headed outside to the porch.

It was dark. The soft lamps at the edge of the driveway gave off enough illumination that she could see shadows without substance. Not the scary kind, thank the Goddess. Besides, she would recognize *that* voice anywhere.

She walked down the steps and met him halfway. "Jared?"

He smiled and her stomach did a teensie-weensie somersault. "Good job today," he said. "I watched."

She smiled back, thinking of all the really cool things that had happened today. It would be hard to pick the coolest, but she had a feeling this could be up in the top five. "Thanks. Congratulations to your sister too. She got the crown. Now you're royalty."

"Not me. Janet. Just because we're twins doesn't mean we are exactly alike."

"Really?"

He stepped closer. "Yeah. You know, it took me a while to figure out what you could *really* be upset about."

Rhiannon felt the dip of her good mood. She tightened her lips and said, "Janet said, and I'm quoting, here, 'my brother

Brian made a bet that Jared could—'"

"You don't have to finish the sentence." Jared's face was red in the soft light.

"So, it's true?"

"Yeah. But you were right about me not taking the bet. Brian's home from college for the weekend and he's got sex on the brain. It doesn't help that he's a moron."

She laughed.

"And Janet can be a pain in the butt. But she's nothing that you can't handle, Rhee. So I asked around. Tried to find out what might make you tick."

Rhiannon dropped her chin from combat level. "You were asking around about me?"

"I found out that you don't trust my family." Jared lifted her hair from her cheek. "I don't blame you."

Her heart raced.

"And that you're worried I might hurt you."

"Who told you that?" Rhee asked with a squeak.

"I can't promise that you'll never be hurt, but I swear that I will do my best to always be honest. I've never known someone like you. Want to try to go on a real date? To the movies or something? Just us."

His face turned brighter red and Rhiannon's doubts disappeared.

Should she tell him that she had the power to crush his stupid twin, or should she just study extra hard and learn to balance her emotions and her logic?

"Not going to answer, huh?" He stammered, "I, uh, brought a present..."

Rhee decided that Jared's only crime was having crappy

siblings. Made her glad she was an only child. She promised herself then and there to learn everything she could from the institute about control. She didn't ever want to hurt him either, or Janet. By the Goddess, Rhee would be happy to never hurt anybody again. "Bribery usually works well for me. I'm a sucker for gifts."

That's when she realized that Jared's jacket was squirming.

He pulled out an orange tabby kitten that had a silver bow around his neck. "For you."

Rhiannon figured the butterflies could just move on into her stomach permanently. She *so* liked this guy. "A real kitten!"

She accepted the wiggling bundle of fur and then stepped into Jared's outstretched arms, the kitten held carefully between them. "Okay. This is definitely worth a movie, but you still have to buy popcorn."

Rhee lifted her face and he brushed her cheek with his fingertips. "With the light shining behind you, you look just like that lady you're named after."

"What?" Rhiannon asked with surprise.

"I did some research. Rhiannon is the moon goddess in Celtic legend. Some branches of the Wiccan religion follow the Celtic mythology, while others follow the Roman influence."

Oh, man. Had she been dumb, or what? "You've been busy. How long have you known?"

"The first day I met you. Your mom kinda gave it away."

Rhiannon let him pull her into a tighter hug. He hadn't told the whole school that her family was Wiccan, not even when he was mad at her. She would return the favor and keep his ancestor's secret safe too. After all, why should he have to pay for the sins of old Abediah?

"I can't believe you know the meaning of my name and

don't laugh every time you say it."

Her heart melted when he stumbled over the words, "But Rhiannon, that's *you*. A goddess."

Rhiannon kissed him full on the mouth before saying, "Nah. I'm still in training."

About the Author

Traci Hall is new to the YA publishing world—but far from new when it comes to understanding the teen brain—which is most complex. ☺

Having barely survived being a teenager, Traci decided to raise them as well. Character studies, their feeding habits, and even their lack of hearing skills, has challenged her in ways she never imagined when the bunny, er, died.

Happily married *forever* to the same great guy, who shares Traci's dedication to reliving the worst of their teen years, Traci has two teenagers, an Xbox, Playstation, and wireless internet for all five of their computers. Traci spends a fortune on those chicken soups that you just need to add water to (minus the veggies, of course) and Cream Soda. Easy Mac, brownies and delivery pizza make up the rest of the menu at Chez Hall. At any given time there are four to twenty teens just hangin' out.

She wouldn't have it any other way!

Please feel free to contact her, or snoop into her biz, at the following web addresses!

www.tracihall.com

www.traciehall.com

www.babesinbookland.com

www.myspace.com/tracihall

Love bites when a seventeen-year-old vampire and witch tangle.

The Vampire...In My Dreams
© *2007 Terry Lee Wilde*

Marissa Lakeland faces her worst nightmare one dark and misty night when she chases a gorgeous hunk of a guy to prove he's a vampire. So why does the thought of tall, dark and vampiric appeal to Marissa, when there's no way a vampire can compel a witch to do his bidding? At least that's what she's read in vampire lore. But lore can be mistaken.

Fledgling vampire Dominic Vorchowski knows Marissa's the only one who can save him. Only why does she have to be a witch? Fate has thrown him together with the bewitching Marissa and if he gains her trust, he'll have his life back again. Except for that whole eternal thirst for blood thing. And the fangs. Not to mention the aversion to intense sunlight. In any event, he's set his sights on one girl who's totally off the menu.

The centuries-old vamp Lynetta wants Dominic to replace the lover she lost, and no teenaged witch is going to take her guy away. Dominic and Marissa must stop the vampiress from winning the battle of the night...but time is running out.

Available now in ebook and print from Samhain Publishing.

GREAT cheap FUN

Discover eBooks!

THE FASTEST WAY TO GET THE HOTTEST NAMES

Get your favorite authors on your favorite reader, long before they're out in print! Ebooks from Samhain go wherever you go, and work with whatever you carry—Palm, PDF, Mobi, and more.

Samhain
publishing ltd

WWW.SAMHAINPUBLISHING.COM

MAY 1 4 2009

Printed in the United States
141033LV00002B/25/P

9 781605 041049